THE YESTERTIME SHIFT

A Novel of Time Travel

YESTERTIME SERIES

Book Four

Andrew Cunningham

Copyright © 2023 by Andrew Cunningham
All Rights Reserved

No portion of this book may be reproduced in any form without written permission from the publisher or author, except as permitted by U.S. copyright law.
ISBN-9798867798253

Books by Andrew Cunningham

Thrillers
Deadly Shore

Alaska Thrillers
Wisdom Spring
Nowhere Alone

Yestertime Time Travel Series
Yestertime
The Yestertime Effect
The Yestertime Warning
The Yestertime Shift

"Lies" Mystery Series
All Lies
Fatal Lies
Vegas Lies
Secrets & Lies
Blood Lies
Buried Lies
Sea of Lies

Eden Rising Series
Eden Rising
Eden Lost
Eden's Legacy
Eden's Survival

Children's Mysteries (as A.R Cunningham)
The Arthur MacArthur Mysteries: The Complete Series

To Charlotte … always

Prologue

INTERPOL HEADQUARTERS—2116

The knock on his door was tentative. The knock on his door was almost always tentative—and it didn't matter who was doing the knocking.

"What?" said the director in a tone that had become all too familiar to his staff.

The door opened.

"Excuse me," said his second-in-command, probably the only person the director trusted fully. "I think I have some good news."

"There is no good news. There's never any good news."

The assistant director looked at his boss. In the last ten years, the man had aged twice that much. His once robust frame was now thin as a rail, and he was always sweating. His desk drawers were filled with anti-anxiety medications, and the man regularly went on weekend benders.

"This may actually be good news."

They had worked long enough together that his assistant no longer had to call him "sir" when they spoke.

The director waved him to go on.

"Our contact inside the NSA just passed on something interesting. Something we might be able to use to solve our problem."

"Oh?"

"As you know, the NSA is closing down the Time Travel Project. In connection with that, it seems they are sending a group of assassins back in time—they call them Eliminators—to kill time travelers. To 'eliminate' them, as they refer to it. They think it's too dangerous to have all those people drifting through time."

"No shit. It's what we've been dealing with for the last ten years. How do they expect to find them?"

"You know the Portal Finders? The instruments the travelers use to find the various portals?"

"Of course."

"Something new has been added—the ability to track the travelers. It's still fairly rudimentary, but it works. Anyone going through a portal picks up some residue. These new Portal Finders can track that residue."

"So, are you saying that these Eliminators might be able to find and kill our man?"

"In theory. But I have a better idea. Why don't we appropriate some of these new Portal Finders and send back a team to kill our guy. No one else. Just our guy."

The director sat up straight. This had possibilities.

"They've never found a way to bring the time travelers back," he said. "How do we convince people to do this job?"

"Outside of the Time Travel Project, the NSA, and the two of us, nobody knows that," said the assistant. "Nobody knows anything about time travel or The Project. It's been a well-kept secret. So, we let these men in on the secret. We offer them a lot of money. We'll find men greedy enough—and dare I say, stupid enough—to do it. They don't have to know that they will never collect on it. Once our people track and find him, they'll kill him, and our nightmare will end. We can pick a spot where the person who kills him can leave the documentation."

"Do it. Steal the Portal Finders. Hire as many men as you need. The more, the better. Put some money in their accounts to seal the deal. We can always take it back later. Offer a gigantic bonus to the man who kills him. It doesn't matter how much because they'll never collect on it."

"I'm on it."

Once his assistant was gone, the director sat back and wiped his face. For the first time in ten years, there was hope. When their former operative accessed the portal and left the message that he was going back to kill the director's ancestors, the director was just waiting for the day he would cease to exist.

What would it feel like? Would he know that he was disappearing? Would he be here one day and gone the next?

For ten years, he had lived with the fear. It had consumed his every waking hour.

Now, for the first time, there was a glimmer of light in his nightmarish life.

PART ONE

Chapter 1

NORTH CONWAY, NEW HAMPSHIRE—AUGUST 15, 2026

"Kind of spooky," said Alice, unsuccessfully removing a cobweb from her face. Every time she pulled one off, another would appear.

"It's meant to be spooky," said Pete. "Why else did you come?"

"It was just a comment, that's all. Sometimes you're a pain in the butt."

"Just part of my appeal."

"Enough," said Keith. "Let's appreciate what we have here."

Keith Miller was the group's leader because of his experience as an urban explorer, and the fact that the others were paying him for his expertise. This was Keith's fourteenth abandoned building and tenth as a paid urbex guide.

This wasn't his life's dream, but it supplemented his income. Keith had been in the infantry in Iraq and had fought in numerous battles and skirmishes. He was always impressed with the work the medics did and vowed to do that for a living. He had become an EMT and was waiting for acceptance to paramedic school. But for now, the extra money came in handy.

He observed his team in the gloom of the building's sagging hallway. Three of them, Pete Green, Alice Firth, and Barbara Cox, were all twenty-four—about ten years younger than Keith. The last member, Nicholas Gates, was in his mid-fifties. He was tall and thin and had a somewhat fragile appearance. But he had signed the paper verifying that he was in good health, so Keith let him join.

Alice, Barbara, and Pete were graduate students and friends at Harvard. Sometimes, the people Keith took out were students in related fields, like urban planning, but this group was just in it for the thrills—the type of group that Keith constantly vowed never to guide again.

It wasn't that they were disruptive or disrespectful; they just didn't appreciate the history of these places. If they wanted thrills, they should have gone to an amusement park.

Well, he could do nothing about it now—he'd already accepted their money.

Barbara took off her helmet.

"It's too hot. We should have waited until fall when it would be cooler."

"Put the helmet back on, please," said Keith. "I made that clear in the beginning—helmets on at all times. You could fall through these rotted floors, or a beam could come down on your head."

"Sorry," mumbled Barbara, putting her helmet back on. "It just seems a little overboard with the safety measures."

"You won't say that when you crack your head against something," answered Keith. "Just keep it on, please."

Keith sighed. There was always one like Barbara, who thought herself tougher than she really was. In fact, this group wasn't much different from most of the other groups, personality-wise. There always seemed to be a tough female and a macho male—Barbara and Pete. Alice was a typical "afraid of the dark" personality who came along simply out of peer pressure. He'd had males and females similar to her in almost every group.

He hadn't figured out Nicholas yet, but the man seemed attentive and interested.

The building Keith had picked for this exploration was on the outskirts of North Conway, in the White Mountains of New Hampshire. Once a popular tourist destination for skiers, the hotel went out of business in the mid-1960s. The disappearances of five people in twelve years gave the hotel a haunted reputation—or, if nothing else, the appearance of the stomping ground of a serial killer. Although the hotel's owners disputed the serial killer theory since no bodies were ever found, no one could dispute the five disappearances. All five were hotel employees, which gave even more credence to the theory that it was a local serial killer.

After the business went under, the owners of the land left the hotel to waste away. Investors had recently bought the property, and the hotel was scheduled for demolition in a week, so Keith needed to explore it now, and he couldn't wait until fall. The building would be long gone by then.

As usual, Keith hadn't asked permission from the owners. There was no way they would approve it—the liability was too great.

"Where are we right now?" asked Nicholas.

"I believe this is the floor used for housing the help."

"They stayed at the hotel?" asked Alice.

"They had to," answered Keith. "There wasn't much else around here. For the hotel to function, they needed to house most of their employees."

"Nothing much on this floor," said Pete.

"I agree. Let's head upstairs. Remember, there are sure to be rotted boards. Stay to the edge of the steps and attached to the rope. If someone falls through, the rest of us can pull them up."

Keith led the way, followed by Alice, Barbara, and Nicholas. Pete was last in line.

The going was treacherous, leading Keith to question his

decision to go upstairs. Rotted boards were everywhere, and twice, he almost went through. He was about to turn the group around when he heard a cry and a crash from the back of the line.

Pete!

The rope pulled everyone back, and then suddenly, the tension disappeared.

"Pete, are you okay?"

No answer.

"Are you on the basement floor?"

"Keith, you have to see this," called out Nicholas.

Keith carefully moved past the two women. In the gloom, Nicholas was holding something. It was the end of the rope.

"Pete detached himself?" asked Keith.

"Look at it," said Nicolas, "it's an even cut—like it was sliced by something very sharp."

Keith shone his flashlight down the hole. Nothing. It was an empty room.

"Pete?" His voice echoed in the room below.

"Follow me," he said to the others, "but be careful."

They stepped around the hole and climbed down the stairs to the hallway they had just left, Keith guided them to the cellar stairs.

"These are concrete but watch yourselves anyway."

They reached the cellar and hurried over to where Pete would have gone down, but there was no room—just a concrete wall.

Keith looked up, hoping he had miscalculated, and he would see a hole above him.

Nothing.

"Where's the door?" asked Alice.

"Maybe on the other side of the room," said Nicholas. "It's odd, though, that there isn't a door on this side."

While they talked, Keith looked around the cluttered basement until he found what he was looking for—a sledgehammer.

"Watch out," he said as he returned to the group.

They got out of his way as he swung the hammer. The wall shuddered.

"It's not too thick," he said.

Two more blows, and he had a hole. The others helped him create a doorway from the crumbling concrete. He called out Pete's name, but there was no response.

"Okay," he said, "let's go in."

"Why don't I go first?" suggested Nicholas.

"No, that's okay," replied Keith, "I'll take the lead."

"Then, can I suggest we hold onto each other?" said Nicholas. "We're connected by the rope, but this might give us all more of a feeling of security."

"Yeah," said Keith. "Good idea."

Alice and Barbara murmured their agreement, and they all carefully stepped over the concrete to the room inside.

Something was immediately wrong. Keith heard music—a tinny waltz.

"Keith?" said Barbara slowly. "Look, where we just came in is all built up again. How can that be? And it's not concrete."

Keith looked around in amazement. The concrete walls and floor were now wood, and the room was no longer empty. Boxes and barrels filled the small space. Some of the boxes contained bottles of alcohol, and others were open bins piled high with potatoes.

"I don't understand. It can't be."

Leading to the outside was a flimsy wooden door.

"It seems to be some kind of root cellar and storage room," said Nicholas.

"And it's being used," said Keith. "This is really strange."

"There's fresh air coming through the door," said Nicholas. "I wonder if Pete came through here. I guess he had to."

"But where is he?" said Barbara.

"And where's the music coming from?" asked Alice. "It sounds right above us, but that's impossible."

"I guess we should go out," said Keith. He was scared. There was something very wrong here.

They no longer held hands, and it seemed stupid to continue to be connected by the rope, so they unclipped themselves.

"I'll go first," said Keith. He hesitated, then lifted the latch on the door and stepped outside. He stood there in disbelief.

It was snowing.

What had just happened?

Chapter 2

NEAR BOSTON—2026

"Ray Burton."

These days, I always answered my phone with a degree of trepidation. Was it going to be a death threat, a wacko wanting to know how they can time travel, or a legitimate call?

"Uh, hi." There was a hesitation. It was a woman's voice. She wasn't sure where to go from there.

"Can I help you?"

"Uh, I'm told you find lost people."

"Well, not really," I said with a sigh. I was getting used to this. "I don't exactly find lost people. I investigate mysterious disappearances."

"That's what I mean. My husband disappeared a week ago. He just vanished."

This was a familiar story. A spouse would take off, leaving the remaining spouse to assume their loved one had gone through a time portal. It was the downside of us telling the world about the portals. Usually, the spouses just wanted to escape a suffocating relationship and start a new life anonymously. Unwilling to admit that something was wrong with the marriage, the remaining spouse now had the excuse of a time portal swallowing up their loved one. In a sad way, it was kind of funny. The chances of going through a portal were far less likely than being struck by lightning or winning the lottery.

"Have you been to the police?" I asked.

"Of course I have. They can't help me."

"And why is that?"

"I told you—because he vanished. He didn't leave any clues. And he wasn't alone. He was with four other people, and they all vanished."

Okay, she had my attention now.

"What's your name?" I asked.

"Cyndi Miller. My husband is Keith Miller. You may have seen it on the news. They found his car, but there was no trace of them."

I knew who she was talking about, and unlike most of the callers I got, I could inform her that she had probably contacted the right person—not that it would make her feel any better. My gut feeling was that her husband and the people he was with wouldn't be returning anytime soon.

Or at all.

Chapter 3

We had been back almost a year.

I'm not sure what I expected once we got home. That I would fall into my old life? That I would take a nice long rest? I knew what we presented to the world would be controversial, but somehow, I retained the illusion that life would return to some semblance of normalcy.

However, it didn't take me long to realize that I could never go back to who I was before. After all, I had just had the experience of a lifetime—or several lifetimes—after running across the chest in the cave that sent me on the most bizarre road trip one could ever take.

So, I had to reinvent myself. I had spent many years as a hotshot journalist, visiting war-torn countries and drug-infested hellholes, before finally burning out. I had teamed with my fellow time traveler Hal March to write the story of our adventures. Despite me having once been the correspondent, Hal was more into the writing of it than I was. I started the book when Natalie and I were living in Saxmundham, England, in the late 1950s. Hal had now taken over the project.

I had gone in a slightly different direction. While Hal was into sharing our experiences, the investigative journalist in me was more interested in the other people who had disappeared.

Thousands of people went missing every year. How many of those were genuinely missing? How many had gone through a time portal?

The answer to the last question was *very few*. Most disappearances were intentional—a way to escape a bad situation. Others were accidental, such as drownings. Then you got into the dark areas—murder and abduction. That left a tiny fraction of disappearances that could be attributed to time portals. These were the ones I wanted to find.

Did it mean I wanted to go after them and try to save them, like I did with Natalie? Not on your life! You'd never catch me within twenty feet of a known portal.

What exactly was a "known" portal?

It was a portal that had shown up on a Portal Finder—and only we had access to the Portal Finders. Simone and I were the only ones who used them, however. Natalie wanted nothing to do with portals ever again. I couldn't blame her. She wanted to concentrate on her movie career. And Hal was wrapped up in writing the book. Simone used the Portal Finders, but for scientific purposes. She was studying them to see if they held a clue as to why so many portals were dying. Once robust portals suddenly disappeared with little warning. The scientist in Simone knew that there had to be a logical reason.

In truth, Hal, Natalie, and Simone had all found their way after returning home—Hal with his writing, Simone with her research of the 21st century and study of time portals, and Natalie with her acting. I was the only one who hadn't yet found his calling in his new life, which is why I was researching missing people—it gave me something to do.

Natalie and I were still together and still deeply in love. We just didn't see a lot of each other. She was on a movie set in Toronto at the moment. It was her first movie since returning, and her first in over sixteen years—at least according to the calendar.

In Natalie's aging years, it was more like five. I visited her on location whenever I could, but I was desperate to find my direction, so it was important for me to spend time at home working on it.

I also had to travel a lot, as it was my responsibility to monitor the drop sites for messages from Alex and Hanna, who were keeping us abreast of their life on the road. We had several portals we used for messages in the U.S. and Canada. There were portals in other countries, but I didn't bother checking them. Alex and Hanna would let us know if they were heading in any of those directions.

But now, thanks to Cyndi Miller, I had another trip to make.

Chapter 4

I told Cyndi that I'd call her back. Before talking to her further, I wanted to research the disappearance of her husband and the others on my own. My gut feeling was that they had encountered a time portal, but it was only that—a gut feeling.

I went online to read the story. When I first heard it on the news, a portal was my immediate thought, but I was kind of biased in that direction. Who's to say they didn't drive into a lake or fall into a crevasse? However, the fact that they found Keith's car sort of canceled out the first option. I remembered that they were in the mountains of New Hampshire, but little else.

I didn't get a lot more information online. It seems that Keith Miller was leading a group in an expedition of an old building. They were called urban explorers. I had heard the term but knew little about it. It turned out that urban explorations were a big thing, but most of the explorations were done illegally, as very few building owners gave permission to have someone possibly break their neck and sue the pants off them. Probably because of that, the name of the building wasn't mentioned in the online reports. I'd have to get that from Cyndi.

What if they had gone through a portal? There wasn't much I could do about it. I certainly wasn't going after them. Been there, never wanted to do it again.

First things first. I'd have to grab my Portal Finder.

When we returned from our journey, we debated destroying most of the Portal Finders. We had about a half dozen of them, having taken them from the Eliminators and others. Half of them were the old style, from when the travelers left in 2105. They worked but were pretty useless when compared to the newer ones. The later models—from 2116 and improved in 2136—could track people who had gone through the portals. With each portal they accessed, the travelers picked up some residue. The newer models could detect that residue.

We could have destroyed them, but we didn't for two reasons: 1) They allowed us to stay in contact with Alex and Hanna, who were still in the early part of the last century—1903 at last report. 2) Alex and Hanna had in their possession the Portal Finder that controlled all the other Portal Finders. The original plan was for them to shut it off when we arrived home safely, but then they decided that they needed to keep it alive, just in case there were other travelers out there who relied on their Portal Finders. So, we kept ours, as well.

The problem was where to hide them. Hal and I had people watching us all the time. We couldn't go anywhere without someone taking pictures or following us in their vehicles. Some were paparazzi—low-end, bottom-feeders for the tabloids. And then there were the others. Some looked to be Feds from some branch of the government—probably the NSA, who had given us a lot of trouble in the past. Others were more questionable. There was also a group of time travel deniers, some of whom had sent us pretty explicit letters about what they wanted to do to us.

I didn't worry about Natalie, as she had a bevy of security people to watch her. I also didn't worry about Simone. We had been careful to keep her a secret. If anyone checked into her, since she and Hal were living together, all they would find would be someone named Meriam Smith, originally from Pittsburgh. Hal had used some government contacts to secure her a Social Security card. So, officially, she was Meriam Smith, but we still called her by her real name, Simone.

No, I was worried about Hal and me. We had both taken to carrying handguns with us wherever we went, not that we went a lot of places. Hal was holed up in his house writing the story of our adventures, and I was inside researching missing people and helping Hal when needed. After all, there were things that happened to me and others before Hal came on the scene.

But I became antsy regularly and had to see the outside world. We had both bought houses outside of Boston, and I spent a lot of time walking and visiting the local parks. I also flew out to see Natalie on her movie sets as much as possible. The rest of the time, I was behind closed doors.

Because of all the focus on security, we had to be extra careful with the Portal Finders. I kept one of the newer models in a safe in my house, and Hal did the same. It was the one Simone used for research. The other Portal Finders were hidden in a storage locker under an assumed name. We stuffed the locker full of worthless junk and hid the Portal Finders deep down in the junk.

I hadn't found much need to use a Portal Finder until now. Most of my research could be done without one. However, the case of Keith Miller was different, and a Portal Finder would be necessary.

I dialed Cyndi Miller's number. She answered on the first ring.

"Mr. Burton?"

"You can call me Ray. Do you know the name of the building your husband was exploring?"

"The Mountain Vista Inn. It was a few miles outside of North Conway. I think they've already torn it down, though."

"That's okay. I don't need the building."

"Do—do you think they went through a time portal?"

"I don't know, Cyndi. I'm going to check it out. Then I'll have a better idea once I get up there."

"And you'll let me know?"

"Absolutely."

"Mr. Bur—Ray, I hated Keith's hobby. I hated it more when he turned it into a part-time business. But I guess the money he was making finally convinced me to accept it. I thought it was dangerous. But I was worried about him falling or getting hit with something. I would never have dreamed of this. Please tell me something. If he did go through a time portal, is there any chance I'll ever see him again?"

"Cyndi, why don't you let me go up and investigate it first before jumping to any conclusions."

"Please. Please be honest with me. I know you still need to go there, but *if* he did go through a portal, will he ever come home?"

I knew this question was coming, but I still wasn't prepared for it. Do I lie or be honest with her? There was only one answer.

"Okay, I'll be honest. If, and I repeat, *if* he went through the portal, no, the chances of him returning are slim at best."

"But you did it."

"We did. But we also had some equipment to help us, and the advice of some travelers we met along the way."

I had to get off the phone.

"Let me scope out the situation. I'll have a much better understanding after I see for myself."

"Okay. I'm sorry to be so whiny, but I love Keith."

"I understand. I'll call you as soon as I can."

I disconnected the call.

Maybe looking for missing people wasn't such a good idea after all.

Chapter 5

Now, to get out of there without being seen.

I dialed Hal.

"You up for a bait and switch?" I asked.

"I sure am. I'll be there in a few minutes."

It was a trick we had tried a few times with good results. Hal would pick me up and drive me to a parking garage in downtown Boston. He would enter the garage, and I would get out on one of the parking levels. Then he'd wait for my signal before leaving. Meanwhile, I would take the stairs to the ground level. When I was sure no one was watching, I'd run across the side street to another parking garage where we kept a nondescript sedan. I would text Hal, and he'd drive out the way he came. I'd wait about ten minutes, then leave my garage. We did this for each other, but I took advantage of it more often than Hal did.

I put some items in a bag, then went to the safe, took out the Portal Finder, and added it to the bag. I almost hated looking at it, as it brought back memories of being lost in time. On the other hand, it got us home.

Not all our travels were bad. Natalie and I were happy living in Saxmundham, England, in the late 1950s until we got bored of it. Perth, in Western Australia in 1902, had its moments, too, but not like Saxmundham. Sadly, many scary times, lonely times, and violent times superseded the good periods. Too many people died, including friends. We couldn't wait to get home.

I saw Hal pull up. I left the house and got in the car. Simone was in the front passenger seat, so I got in the back.

"Thank you," I said.

"Happy to do it. And it's always nice to get out of the house."

"Hi, Simone."

"Hi, Ray. Hal and I might even take this time to go for lunch. We've been cooped up for too long."

"Where are you off to?" asked Hal.

"New Hampshire. We might have some travelers."

Hal March was in his early sixties—about ten years older than me. He had once owned an antiques magazine business. Unbeknownst to him at the time, a couple of time travelers had worked for him, which is how I got to know him. We hit it off immediately, and when I went back in time to help Natalie, Hal was my contact on the "other side," so to speak. When the NSA decided to eliminate anyone with knowledge of the NSA's interest in time travel, Hal had to run for his life—right to a portal and another time. He managed to meet up with Natalie and me, and along with Alex, Hanna, and Simone, we had some dangerous adventures together.

When we met Simone—part of the original group of travelers, along with Hanna, in the Time Travel Program from the next century—she was fragile, having endured ten years of abuse in a French mental hospital in the 1700s. Over time, she began to heal, but it was a long process. She wasn't there yet but was getting closer. Hal was much older than Simone, but they were devoted to each other.

On the way to the parking garage, I told them about my phone call from Cyndi Miller.

"You're right," said Hal, "it sounds like it could be travelers."

"What are you going to do?" asked Simone.

"I'm not sure. My whole reason for getting involved with this was to track down possible travelers from the comfort of my computer and document them. It was never my intention—nor will it be—to try to save anyone. I think the most I can do here is to prove it one way or another. Either they went through a portal, or they didn't. Then I can give the information to Cyndi Miller. At least she'll know what happened."

I threw my hands in the air.

"Hey, I'm making this up as I go along."

I counted three cars following us—that was fewer than usual. Could it be that they were losing interest? I could only hope.

We drove into the garage, and I got out on the fifth floor.

"Good luck, and don't go through any portals," said Hal. It was our usual way of saying goodbye.

I descended the garbage-strewn stairs, which reeked of urine, and crossed to the other garage. I texted Hal, and a few minutes later, I was on my way to New Hampshire.

It was a long way up to North Conway, but it was a pleasant drive once I got away from the city. Though with such a long ride, I'd probably have to find a hotel for the night in North Conway.

First, I had one stop to make. After confirming that the switch had worked and I wasn't being followed, I stopped at the storage facility and went to our unit. It took a while to get through all the junk—which was how we planned it—but I finally reached the extra Portal Finders. I picked out one of the older models and put it in a bag. I fought my way back to the unit's entrance. I locked it and was back on my way a few minutes later.

About an hour into the drive, I got a call from Natalie, who was on a break. She was checking in, so I told her my mission.

"Stay far away from the portal," she said.

"Don't worry. I have the Portal Finder with me. I won't get within yards of it."

"Miles from it would be better," said Natalie.

Before I left, I had turned it on and confirmed that there was a portal in the vicinity of North Conway.

"I'm not sure how I feel about you playing around with portals," she said. It wasn't the first time she had made the comment.

"To be honest, I'm not sure either."

"You're still lost, aren't you?" she asked.

"Kind of."

I felt a lump in my throat, and my eyes filled with tears. I was just happy that Natalie couldn't see me. It didn't matter, though, as she sensed it.

"I wish I were there to hug you," she said.

"Me too. How about I fly up this weekend? I just want to be near you."

"I would love that."

"How's the production going?" I asked.

"It's great. I like the director. He treats me like an actor, not a freak show time traveler."

Before accidentally encountering the portal in Hollow Rock, Arizona, Natalie was an award-winning movie actress. But she had tired of the life of a movie star and had planned to retire at the ripe old age of thirty. But now, she couldn't sign up for enough roles.

Natalie had been missing for sixteen years, but she had amazed the world when she returned only five years older—the actual amount of time she had been traveling, biologically speaking.

We talked for a while longer, then promised to speak that night.

I arrived in North Conway about three hours after leaving Boston. I tracked the location to a spot about five miles outside the town using the Portal Finder.

I have to say that it did have a spectacular mountain view.

The hotel's name was no lie. However, there was no hotel. It had been demolished. All that remained was a hole with the concrete walls of the basement. All the piping had been removed, and a gigantic pile of dirt sat at the hole's edge. They were going to fill it in, and soon. This was Friday afternoon, and no one was around, so they had probably finished work for the week. The dirt pile was fresh, and a front-end loader sat beside it. I guessed that it would be filled on Monday morning.

Well, if I was going to contact Keith Miller, it would have to be in the next two days. Otherwise, it wouldn't happen. Once this hole was filled, they were on their own.

I clicked one of the switches on the Portal Finder and immediately picked up the trails of ten people—four were together, and the others were not. The trails would account for Keith and his group, as well as the five people who disappeared over the years. It was interesting, though, that only four of Keith Miller's group were together. The trails were faint and hard to see, as was usually the case with people who had only gone through one portal. While they picked up portal residue, one portal wouldn't provide much. On the other hand, Hanna had been through so many portals her trail almost glowed.

Curiously, though, one of the trails in the party of four was stronger than the others. Why would that be? I took a picture with my phone to show Simone when I returned.

In the past, I might have wondered why the front-end loader or one of the workers demolishing the place hadn't gone through the portal's entrance. But I knew now that you had to enter the portal precisely through the entrance. A tractor would be too large, and a worker would have to hit it at exactly the right place. Granted, some portals were larger than others, but this wasn't one of those.

I looked at the Portal Finder to see where this portal emptied out.

The screen read 1917.

That wasn't good, but it could be worse. Yeah, tell that to the people stuck there.

I returned to my car, opened the bag I had packed, and took out a bright red plastic bottle with a wide mouth. Then I wrote a note on a small pad of paper and put the whole pad and a pencil in the bottle. On the side of the bottle, I wrote *Keith Miller* in thick black marker. Then I carefully lowered myself into the hole and, using the Portal Finder, pinpointed the entrance to the portal.

Staying many feet away, I tossed the bottle into the portal. As it entered the portal, the bottle disappeared.

Now, all I could do was wait.

Chapter 6

NORTH CONWAY, NEW HAMPSHIRE – TIME UNKNOWN

It was a dream. It had to be. Pete hated this kind of dream—the kind that feels real, and you can't wake up from.

But he was fooling himself. This was no dream. This was something else—but what? One minute, he was exploring the old building, then he fell through the floor. He had hit the ground hard and had the wind knocked out of him. Once Pete caught his breath, he called to the others, but they didn't answer. He unclipped his flashlight and shone it at the hole he fell through. What hole? It was gone. No, that couldn't be.

Pete looked around him. He was in a small room piled high with boxes and barrels. There were two bins of loose potatoes. The room was dark and chilly, but he could see through cracks in an old wooden door that it was sunny outside.

He shook his head. It made no sense at all. Maybe he should wait for Keith and the others—they were probably on their way down from the floor above to see how he was. But how would they get to him? The only opening was the door to the outside. Okay, he'd wait for them out in the sun. But it still felt strange. Something wasn't right.

Pete stood up painfully and almost hit his head on the low

ceiling. It was only about six feet high. But that couldn't be. He fell at least fifteen feet—maybe more. He felt his hip. It was bruised, but at least nothing seemed broken. He opened the door and squinted at the bright sun. That was strange. It had been overcast all morning, and they were predicting rain in the afternoon. Now, there wasn't a cloud in the sky. It smelled different, too. It smelled like spring. It was the scent he'd always loved in school. It meant winter was gone, and baseball season had begun.

But how could it smell like that? It wasn't spring—it was the middle of August. That had a completely different smell.

Pete walked out, turned, and looked at the old building.

It wasn't old!

It seemed smaller than when they went in earlier. But that wasn't all. The building was painted a gleaming white, and all around the base were flower beds, with new green stalks just emerging from the dirt.

"What were you doing in our shed?"

He turned around quickly. A squat, middle-aged man wearing blue overalls was staring at him.

"Son, I asked you a question."

Pete was twenty-four but looked younger. He was sometimes mistaken for his late teens. That's why he had started growing a beard. It wasn't very far along yet, but at least he didn't look much like a teenager anymore.

"I'm sorry," he answered. "I'm very confused. This building is supposed to be abandoned. I was just in it, and it was falling apart."

"You were just in it? Falling apart? Son, are you okay? We just built this last year. And I know you weren't in it—well, other than the shed."

Pete shook his head. "Is this the Mountain Vista Inn?"

"The one and the same."

"But—but." Pete suddenly felt hot, and things became hazy.

He dropped to the ground.

*****

When Pete woke up, he was in bed, but it wasn't his bed. This bed was fat and soft—like a feather bed. He was covered with a blanket, and someone was looking at him. It was a man, but not the same man he saw outside.

"Feelin' better?"

"I—I guess. Where am I?"

"You're in the Mountain Vista Inn. The owners were nice enough to give you a room."

"What happened?" Pete asked.

Pete looked at the man more closely. He was dressed in an old-fashioned suit and had a stethoscope hanging around his neck. But even that seemed old-fashioned. It was nothing like the one his doctor at home wore.

"You fainted. Bill and Ruth—they're the owners—were worried about you, so they put you to bed and called me. I'm Doc Billings. Took me a while to get here from town, but you slept the whole time."

"Are my friends here?" asked Pete.

"I can't say. Ruth and Bill, could you come in?"

They must have been waiting outside the door because they were in the room in seconds.

"The young man asked about his friends. You got any of them staying here?"

"We have no guests at the moment," said Ruth. She was a short, middle-aged, matronly woman with a kind face. "We're expecting two couples on the weekend, but we have no guests at the moment."

Pete was confused.

"Weekend? It's Saturday today, isn't it?"

"That fainting spell did something to your head," said Bill. He was the man who had approached him outside. Pete thought he looked like a carbon copy of Ruth. "It's Tuesday."

Tuesday? How could that be? It was Saturday when they started exploring the old building—which now wasn't old. Pete closed his eyes. *Please let me be dreaming.*

"You're not from around here," said Doc Billings. "Where do you hail from?"

"Boston," said Pete. "I was up here with my friends exploring an old building scheduled for demolition. I fell through the floor and ended up in the cellar. I know it sounds strange, but I'm telling the truth."

The others chuckled.

"Sounds like you had quite the dream," said Ruth. "This building is only a year old. I don't think they are tearing it down anytime soon."

"How long have I been asleep?"

"A couple of hours," said Ruth.

For a fleeting second, Pete wondered if he'd been asleep for months, and they built this in place of the old building. But now he didn't know what to think.

"I don't mean to get personal," said Bill, "but why aren't you overseas?"

"Overseas?"

"Fighting for your country."

"Fighting? Fighting where? We pulled out of Iraq and Afghanistan."

"What are you talking about? We're talking about the war."

"The war?"

"Son, have you been living in a cave? The war against the Huns."

Pete must have looked confused because Bill shook his head.

"The Germans."

And then it hit him. Natalie O'Brien and all the talk about time travel. He hadn't believed a word of it. But what if it was true?

"I'm sorry," he said to the others. "You must think I'm simple or something. I suddenly realize what's happening. I'm going to ask you a strange question. What year is it?"

"You're joking," said Bill.

Ruth stepped in front of Bill to answer Pete's question. Putting her hand on Pete's cheek as if he were a simpleton, she answered him in a quiet voice.

"It's 1917."

Chapter 7

NORTH CONWAY, NEW HAMPSHIRE—1917

Pete felt a chill overcome him. It couldn't be.

"So, when you mention the war, you're talking about World War One," said Pete.

"What are you talking about?" asked Doc Billings. "The Great War. The war against the Germans."

The tears came from out of nowhere, and Pete began to shake.

"What the—" said Bill.

"It's okay, dear," said Ruth. "Not everyone is brave enough to go."

Doc Billings just made a face.

"I'm leaving," he said with disgust, and walked out the door.

Meanwhile, Pete was shaking his head at Ruth's comment. He held up his finger to let her know he was about to say something. Pete sniffed a couple of times.

"I'm sorry," he said. "You have no idea what a shock this is. Please sit, and I'll try to explain it."

Instinct told Pete that what he was about to do wasn't smart. But he was all alone. What choice did he have? He had to talk to someone.

Once Ruth and Bill were seated, Pete said, "You're not going to believe what I have to say, but I have to tell you anyway. I'm not a coward, and I'm not simple. I'm a graduate student at Harvard, and I'm as brave as the next guy. But I'm not from here."

"You're from Boston," said Bill. "You told us."

"That's not what I mean. I'm not from this time. A few hours ago, I was in this very building, but it had been abandoned for many years and was about to be torn down."

"You're talking nonsense," said Ruth.

"I come from a different time. I come from the year 2026. That's a hundred and nine years from now."

"You're possessed." Ruth's voice had taken on a different tone. She no longer looked like the kindly woman she had a few minutes earlier.

"No, I can prove it," cried Pete. "I need you to believe me."

Bill and Ruth sat in a stony silence.

"The reason I called this World War One is because, in 1939, Europe goes to war with Germany again. The United States enters it a couple of years later. That's known as World War Two. So, they changed the name of this from "The Great War" to "World War One.""

"Ruth is right," said Bill. "You're possessed. You have demons inside you."

Pete suddenly realized that Bill and Ruth were not the people to hear it. He had made a mistake. But something in him still felt that he needed to prove it to them. He reached into his back pocket for his wallet.

"I have proof," he said.

He pulled out his driver's license. "See? This shows my date of birth. I was born in 2002." He took out his credit cards. "And these are called credit cards. Where I come from, people use them in place of cash. But they still have cash," he added, pulling out a few bills. "Look at the dates on these bills."

Bill asked to see the wallet.

"Sure," said Pete, thinking he might have gotten through to them. He handed Bill the wallet and cash.

Bill stood up and quickly left the room.

"No, I need that back!"

He shakily stood up to go after Bill. Ruth pushed him back onto the bed.

"No, this is for your own good."

Pete was mad now.

"Like hell it is."

He stood up and pushed past her. He had regained his balance and moved fast now. He grabbed his shoes, which they had taken off him before putting him in bed. He turned left in the hall to follow Bill. He sped down the hall and took the stairs to the first floor, two steps at a time. He stopped short when he reached the living room. A fire was blazing in the fireplace. On top of the fire was his wallet, half burning and half melting.

"Noooo!"

"It's for your own good," said Bill, repeating the same line Ruth had used just a minute before. "You're possessed by the devil. Leave this house immediately!"

Pete's wallet was now a melted ball. It was gone.

"I'll leave, you fucking wacko," yelled Pete. "You didn't have to do that to my wallet. Now I have no proof to show sane people."

"I said, leave!"

Pete ran out the front door, sobbing. Any proof of who he was and where he came from was now gone. It was a mistake to try and convince Bill and Ruth. They'd seemed so nice. How was he to know that they were like that?

He walked down the road toward North Conway, his shoes still in his hand. He stopped to put them on. The road wasn't paved, like he remembered it being. Now, it was just a narrow dirt road. He tried to remember how far away the town was. Five miles, maybe? That was okay. He needed the time to clear his head.

He reached into his pocket for his phone. Oh, right, he had left it in Keith's car. He hadn't seen any need for it in the abandoned building.

What could he do now? Telling people where he was from was a bad idea. Maybe others wouldn't be as extreme as Ruth and Bill, but the chances of them believing him were slim, at best—especially since he no longer had proof. He felt like crying again. He moved off the road and sat under a tree. The tears came again—this time with deep sobs.

Pete had never been so scared in his life. Once the crying stopped, he fell asleep against the tree. When he woke up, it was late afternoon. He felt marginally better and knew that if he was going to survive, he'd have to keep his wits about him.

Pete thought about his appearance. His light brown hair was cut relatively short. It probably wouldn't raise any alarms. After all, it wasn't his appearance that set off Ruth and Bill; it was his words. He was wearing work boots. They were probably different from the current style, but he didn't think they would be noticed. He had on a plaid long-sleeve flannel shirt and Levi's. Again, it was nothing radical. They wore flannel shirts and Levi's in 1917. He was sure of it. It was good that he changed out of sneakers at the last minute to explore the building. That was Keith's suggestion. He said the boots were safer. He had also added the flannel shirt at Keith's urging. Although he would be hotter, long sleeves were safer than a t-shirt.

So, where were Keith and the others? Did they come after him? If so, why weren't they right behind him when he landed in the shed?

Then it hit him. Nobody was coming after him.

He was alone in a foreign land.

Chapter 8

Pete was tired of sitting, but he needed a plan. He couldn't go into North Conway without some kind of strategy. The problem was that North Conway was probably much smaller in 1917 than in 2026. Pete could almost guarantee that Doc Billings had already spread the word that a coward was at the Mountain Vista Inn. The minute Pete showed his face in town, everyone would know who he was.

If he could make it to Boston, at least he would be anonymous.

What was he thinking? Was he admitting already that there was no way he could get home—that he was stuck here for the rest of his life? Should he go back to the Mountain Vista Inn and stick around the portal? Portal. That's what Natalie O'Brien called them, if he remembered right. Now, he wished he'd paid more attention to her story. He was so quick to dismiss the tale as a publicity stunt. But that correspondent—what was his name? Burton—he was involved, too. And everyone said that he had a solid reputation. Yes, he was now regretting it.

Was there anything he remembered? Something about portals being one-way only. If that was the case, he couldn't use it to return home. But what if that actress was wrong? What if some of them worked both ways?

He could sneak back at night and try. After all, he had nothing to lose. He was also hungry. He hadn't eaten since breakfast. He almost laughed. *Breakfast 109 years in the future.* That root cellar had boxes of supplies. There was probably something he could eat. If need be, he could eat raw potatoes. There were certainly enough of them.

What about Ruth and Bill? *Screw them. They'll be lucky if I don't set fire to the place.*

There was another reason to go back there. What if the others got caught in the portal? Maybe they couldn't get to him for a while. Maybe they are still going to come out. What if they've already come out?

Suddenly, Pete needed to get back to the portal. The others might be waiting for him, or they might be as confused as he had been. He especially needed to see Barbara—the two of them were close. No, they weren't close—they were in love. What had begun as a night of meaningless sex had progressed into a real love affair. They hadn't told Alice the extent of their relationship, but Pete was pretty sure she had caught on.

Pete wasn't far from the Mountain Vista Inn, so it was within sight in minutes. In case someone was watching from the Inn, he cut across the road into the woods behind the building. He traveled through the woods until he was near the storage shed. Bill called it a shed, but it was attached to the Inn and in the same spot as the cellar, which must have come later. He hid behind some trees and waited for it to get dark.

A couple of times, Pete saw Bill come outside to get something from the shed and then return to the Inn. The second time, Pete was tempted to surprise Bill and beat him senseless for doing what he had done with Pete's wallet. But that wouldn't help his situation, so he waited.

During that time, there was no sign of Keith, Alice, Barbara, or Nicholas.

Signing up with Keith had been his idea. Barbara had latched onto the idea immediately. But then, she would. She was always trying to prove her bravery. The fact that she and Pete were also sleeping together often led to competition between them, resulting in them always trying extreme adventures to outdo each other. Poor Alice was caught in the middle. She didn't like the adventures, but she was Barbara's best friend and didn't like to be left out. They had constantly pressured Alice into joining them.

But maybe this time, they had taken the extreme thing a little too far.

Finally, it was dark. The moon was out, but Pete didn't think it would provide enough light for anyone to see him. When the lights went out in the Inn, it was time to go. He quietly left his hiding spot and went down the small hill behind it. He entered the shed. It was pitch black, so he unclipped his flashlight—at least he still had that—and turned it on. The light was almost too bright. Could they see it from outside? Probably. The door had lots of cracks in it. Well, he'd only keep it on for a minute.

Searching quickly through the boxes, he was disappointed to find nothing to eat. The boxes were filled with bags of flour and sugar and other bulk kitchen cooking items. In the other boxes were dozens of bottles of beer.

I would have thought beer would be considered the drink of demons, he thought.

"I guess it's beer and potatoes," he said.

He wiped off one of the potatoes and bit into it. *It's not half bad,* he thought.

He pulled out one of the beer bottles and examined it with the flashlight. It had a metal lift cap instead of the flip-type he had always seen. Etched into the glass were the words *Registered, P. Harrington Sons, Manchester, NH*. It had the manufacturer's logo, and the date *1917* also etched in the glass.

I bet this would go for big money on eBay, thought Pete.

He turned off the flashlight and got comfortable, drinking beer and eating raw potatoes.

*****

Someone was shaking him, and a light was blinding him.

"Get your sorry ass on your feet."

"Huh, what?"

Pete was trying to figure out what was happening.

"I said, get on your feet, you lousy coward."

Fear ran through Pete's body. He had fallen asleep. It was the beer—he'd had too much of it.

Whoever yelled at him was now pulling him out of the shed. He was thrown to the ground. Two men held lanterns.

"This the kid, Bill?"

"That's him. Had himself a cockamamie story about being from the future. He pretended not to know anything about the war."

"He'll know about it when I'm done with him. C'mon, kid. You're coming with us."

Pete saw badges on their chests reflecting the lantern light. Each took one of Pete's arms and escorted him roughly to a waiting car. It was old. A Model T or maybe a Model A—Pete knew little about cars, and those were the only two that came to mind.

The men pushed him into the car and onto a hard seat.

"I think there's been a misunderstanding," said Pete.

One of the men backhanded him across his face. It hurt—a lot.

"Shut your mouth and don't say another word. We'll deal with you when we get to town."

Pete kept quiet for the rest of the ride. It was dark when they pulled him out of the shed, but the sun was now beginning to emerge over the top of the surrounding mountains. The policemen drove slowly in the dark, the electric headlamps offering only marginal light. As it got brighter outside, the car sped up.

Pete could now see the men clearly. Both were large, with walrus mustaches and thick necks. Pete knew that there would be no escaping them. They arrived in town a little while later. It looked nothing like the town Pete had been in before this nightmare had begun. It wasn't built up, and the roads were a lot wider.

They stopped in front of a square wooden building with a sign that said simply, *Police*.

They pushed him inside and into a cell. The cops entered the outer office and closed the door behind them without a word.

Pete sat on a bunk and looked around. The jail had just two cells, and he was the only guest. It was too late to kick himself, but he could have. He'd had the opportunity to cancel the exploration trip but didn't. He could have taken an overtime shift at the restaurant. It would have meant some good tips. The owners begged him to work it, but he had already paid Keith and didn't want to ask for his money back. If only ....

What were they going to do to him? These guys were mean, and because they thought he was a coward, they would be even meaner toward him.

In some ways, his life was over. He had no idea how to get home, and he was in a place and time that he didn't understand. History had never been his strength, so he couldn't even fake it. And it was too far back in time for him to look up his parents or grandparents—not that he'd know what to do even if he could. What would he say to them?

So, he sat in silence for hours. Finally, at 1:30, according to the clock on the wall, the two cops walked in with another man, who was wearing an ill-fitting military uniform. The man had to be close to 70.

"I'm Sheriff Bud Kush," said the cop in charge. "What's your name?"

"Pete. Pete Green."

"Bill and Ruth said you told them you're from Boston. They also told me you had an outlandish story about being from the future."

"It's not outlandish, and if Bill hadn't stolen my wallet and thrown it in the fire, I could prove it to you. My flashlight. That'll prove it. It's more advanced than anything you have now."

He reached for it, but it was gone. Then he remembered unclipping it when he was in the shed. He must have left it there. He explained it to Sheriff Kush.

"Nice try," said Kush. "So, you have no identification at all? Nothing to prove who you are?"

"Not anymore."

"Then this is your lucky day. From now on, you are Mr. Peter Green of North Conway, New Hampshire." He pointed to the older man in uniform. "And this is Captain Fitz of the Army Reserve. He's going to get you signed up for military service."

"What? I'm not going into the military."

"You don't have to," said Kush, "but the alternative won't be pleasant. You've been accused of attacking two nice people—Bill and Ruth. Once I add a few charges, you'll go to prison for a long time. You have a single cell now, but you sure won't when you get to prison. And your cellmates might not be so nice."

So, that was how it was going to be. He had no choice, and they knew it.

"Now, once you enter the Army, you can always try to escape, but the Army doesn't think highly of cowards. They shoot deserters."

"I'm not a coward. I'm from the future, and as much as you don't want to hear it, it's true. I can tell you who wins this war and the next one. I can tell you all the presidents for the next hundred years."

He couldn't really, but it didn't matter. He knew some of them but could always make up the rest.

He continued before they could interrupt.

"In 1941, the Japanese attack—"

"Shut up!" demanded Kush. "I don't want to hear any more of your bullshit. Captain Fitz has the paperwork. You sign it, or you don't. I don't care. But if you don't, you will regret it for the rest of your life.

Pete had no choice. He signed his induction papers.

"I hit my quota," said Captain Fitz. "Thanks, Sheriff."

"To make sure you don't make a run for it, my deputy will accompany you down to Manchester and the induction center."

Escape was exactly what Pete was planning to do. Now, his final avenue had just dried up.

Pete was joining the Army—in 1917!

Chapter 9

NORTH CONWAY, NEW HAMPSHIRE—LATE 1917

Keith and the others watched in awe as the snow fell around them.

"Keith," said Alice, "I don't understand. What happened? It's so cold."

Alice was shivering. They all were. Keith removed the light jacket he always wore while exploring and put it around Alice's shoulders.

Nicholas, also wearing a jacket, started to take it off to give to Barbara, but she held up her hand.

"I'm fine."

Nicholas could tell she wasn't, but he wouldn't force it on her.

Barbara, tanned, with dark hair and a small dragon tattoo on her neck, looked to Nicholas like she worked out regularly. Staying fit seemed to match her cocky personality. Alice was the opposite, with light skin and blonde hair. Her pale complexion seemed to match her timidness. She had a nice body but lacked the muscle tone that Barbara displayed. Alice sported a thin nose ring. *Maybe it's her one bit of rebellion,* thought Nicholas.

Nicholas knew what had happened. In fact, he had anticipated going through it himself. What he didn't anticipate was being joined by the others. He should have stopped them. He tried by offering to go first, but Keith shot that down. What more could he have done?

Were they prepared for this? Alice certainly wasn't. Behind her bluster, he wasn't sure Barbara was either. Keith? He was older than the others, so maybe he could handle it better. He looked capable. Nicholas guessed that Keith was former military. He was clean-cut, with short brown hair, and looked like he worked out regularly. He could probably deal with most things thrown his way.

But Nicholas doubted that any of them were prepared for this.

Keith looked up at the building behind them. It was similar to the decrepit building they had been in but was newer and smaller. At some point in the future, two more floors would be added.

"How did this get here?" asked Barbara.

"Something happened to us," said Alice. "It's like we've gone someplace else."

"Maybe we have," said Nicholas. "I know this sounds farfetched, but there's been a lot in the news over the last year about time travel, ever since Natalie O'Brien showed up after being missing for sixteen years."

"That's bullshit," said Barbara. "That was publicity crap. She was probably in rehab all those years."

"I think there's something to it," said Alice, her teeth chattering between words.

"I'm afraid there's a lot to it," said Keith. He had wandered from the group for a minute. "I just looked around the corner of the building. There's a sign that says Mountain Vista Inn. I—"

He bit off the end of the sentence because he felt tears coming, and he didn't want to cry in front of the others. There was no doubt in Keith's mind that they had just accessed a time portal. From what he had read, they were only one-way. Was that true? If so, they would never get home. He thought of Cyndi.

"No," said Barbara. "I refuse to believe it. It's gotta be something else."

"Like what?" asked Nicholas. "You give me a logical explanation."

"I don't have one. I'm just saying that it's not time travel."

Listening to her, Keith thought Barbara seemed slightly less convinced than she had a minute earlier.

"Let's try going back in the portal—if that's what it is," suggested Keith. "I heard they were one-way, but what if this one isn't?"

They all entered the shed, but nothing changed.

"Hey, look at this," said Alice, picking up a bright red plastic container. "It wasn't here before. Oh my God! Keith, it has your name on it."

"What?"

Alice handed it to him. He looked at the others, then carefully unscrewed the top. He pulled out a pad of paper.

"It's a note written to me."

He read it aloud.

Keith,

My name is Ray Burton. You may have heard of me. I'm writing this in vague language in case it's not you who finds it. I have something that might be able to help you get home—but there are no guarantees, unfortunately.

I only have a short window of time to write you these notes, but fortunately, on your end, time is relative. Where you are, it might take you several months to get this message and any subsequent ones, but I should get your responses immediately.

Before I get into specifics, please respond to this—but don't put it back in the portal, or I won't be able to retrieve it. I looked around for a good message site. About a half mile down the road is a covered bridge.

The sign on it says it was built in 1886, so it will be there in 1917, which is where you landed. On the left side of the end closest to you, are a lot of rocks. Hide the container among the rocks. Hide it well so the red can't be seen, and so it will last 109 years. Please include your wife's name somewhere in the note, so I know it's you. When I get your response, I will send you the container back through the portal and will attach something to it. As I said, it might not appear right away, but it might. It could take months, so please be patient. Time is a confusing concept. If it doesn't immediately appear, you will have to keep checking the spot so no one else finds it.

I feel for you and know exactly what you're going through. Just try to stay positive.

Ray

"Someone knows we're here," said Alice.

"Is this a joke?" asked Barbara. "Did someone pay you to create a massive joke at my expense?" She was shaking now.

"Barbara," said Nicholas. "I can assure you that this isn't a joke. I wish it were. Ray Burton was the guy who traveled through time with Natalie O'Brien. As much as I don't want this to be real, it is."

"He says we're in 1917," said Alice. "Could that be true?"

"It most likely is," said Nicholas.

"I suspected this but hoped I was wrong," said Keith.

"Me too," said Nicholas. "But if there's a way to get out of here, we need to follow his directions. You write the note, and I'll take it to the bridge. I'll do a good job of hiding it."

Keith started writing:

Ray,

Thank you for finding us. It's very scary, as I'm sure you remember. There were five of us, but Pete Green went through before us. He fell through some rotted wood into the portal. We don't know where he is.

We would appreciate anything you can do for us.
Please tell my wife, Cyndi, that I love her.
Keith

He sealed the note in the container and gave it to Nicholas, who jogged to the road.

"We need to get warm," said Keith. "Maybe they'll let us warm up inside."

Keith had barely gotten those words out of his mouth when he heard a shout.

"Hey, what are you people doing here?"

Think fast, Keith. Think fast.

"We're looking for a friend of ours who's gone missing." *Better to stay close to the truth.*

The man was about fifty feet away. He had just rounded the corner of the building. He took a step closer and adjusted his glasses.

As if one step will make a difference, thought Keith.

The man looked to be in his early fifties and was short and round. He was also carrying a shotgun.

"My name is Keith. This is Alice and Barbara. Nice to meet you."

"Uh-huh," said the man. "Name's Bill." He took a couple of steps closer.

"Hi, Bill," said Keith. "We're looking for a friend. His name is Pete. We think he might have come this way. We were hoping that you might have seen him."

"Saw him. You people from Boston?"

"We are."

"Are you going to tell me some crazy story about coming from the future?"

What would Ray Burton do?

"From the future? Is that what Pete told you?" asked Keith.

Wrong move, Pete, he thought.

"He did. The boy didn't seem stable."

"I'm afraid he's not. That's why we need to find him. He has some problems."

"Well, you're too late."

Alice gasped.

"Why are we too late?" asked Barbara.

"Your friend joined the Army," said Bill.

He adjusted the shotgun.

"He's on his way to France."

Chapter 10

"What?" exclaimed Keith. "How?"

"He got himself in a spot of trouble. The sheriff gave him a choice of going to prison or joining the Army. Your friend is now a doughboy."

"Doughboy?" asked Alice.

"Yeah, doughboy. Are you as dense as your friend?"

"Hey," said Keith. "Do you talk like that to everybody, or are you just a dumb hick who doesn't know better?"

Keith felt safe in saying that because he saw Nicholas coming up behind Bill.

"How dare you—" started Bill. As he brought his gun up, it was snatched from his hands. He turned to face Nicholas, who struck him in the stomach with the butt of the shotgun.

"Nooo. Leave him alone!"

A woman who looked remarkably like Bill came running around the corner of the building.

"Don't hurt him."

Nicholas turned and pointed the shotgun at her. She stopped in her tracks.

"Nicholas, don't," said Keith.

"Well, we're in kind of a predicament," replied Nicholas.

"Still, you don't need to do that."

Nicholas lowered the gun.

"What's your name?" asked Keith.

"Ruth," she said shakily.

Bill stood up with a groan but was still bent over in pain.

"We're not going to hurt you," said Keith, "but we need a place to stay. How many guests do you have?"

"Well, none. It's winter." She said it as if she were talking to an idiot.

"I guess skiing hasn't caught on yet," Barbara whispered to Alice.

"So you don't expect anyone soon?" asked Keith.

"Not until spring," Ruth answered warily.

"Then you have some guests now," said Keith. "We need a place to stay for a short time. We won't hurt you or your husband—"

"He's my brother."

"That explains why they look alike," said Nicholas. To Ruth, he said, "What Keith means to say is that we won't hurt you *if* you don't try to contact anyone or attempt to escape."

Bill gave Nicholas daggers with his eyes but nodded his head in agreement.

Nicholas handed Keith the shotgun.

"I never got to the spot." He was careful not to say bridge. "I saw this guy come around the corner and figured I'd better wait."

"Good thing," said Keith. "Thanks."

"I'll be back in a little while."

"Let's all go inside," said Keith. "My name is Keith. This is Alice and Barbara. The other man is Nicholas. We're going to be your guests for a while. I'm afraid we have no choice."

Neither Bill nor Ruth responded.

Inside was warm and cozy, with a roaring fire in the living room fireplace.

"This is very nice," Alice said to Ruth.

"Thank you," Ruth said sullenly. But her face showed that she was happy with the comment.

Nicholas showed up an hour later, nodding to Keith that his mission was successful. Knowing they had no choice, Ruth showed them to their rooms. There were three guest rooms, but the group felt safer doubling up—Keith and Nicholas shared one room, and Alice and Barbara another.

Alice offered to help Ruth with dinner. Alice was determined to show the brother and sister that it would all be okay. Ruth grudgingly agreed to her offer.

At dinner, Keith decided to speak to make the situation clear to their hosts.

"We are all sorry for the intrusion—truly, we are. This was never our intention. In fact, we never intended to be anywhere near here. But circumstances have dictated it. We're all nice people, but we're nice people in a tough situation."

"What's your situation?" asked Bill.

"Can't tell you that."

"Damn it!" Bill yelled, slamming his fist on the table.

"Bill, watch your language," admonished Ruth.

But Bill chose not to hear her.

"You come into our home and hold us prisoner. You say you're nice people, but you're not. You have a situation but refuse to tell us what it is. Meanwhile, we have to sit by and watch you take over our home for God knows how long. It's not fair!"

Bill's face had turned beet red.

Keith looked over at Nicholas, then at the women. They all nodded their consent to the obvious question.

"Okay, I'll tell you what our situation is. But first, tell me how Pete ended up in the Army."

Bill explained about Pete's arrival, telling them he was from the future, getting caught by the police, and then given the choice by the sheriff to go to prison or join the Army.

"The boy was a coward. He was shirking his responsibilities."

"He's not a coward!" said Barbara, leaning over the table and getting in Bill's face. "Pete's braver than you'll ever be."

"So it really wasn't a choice to join the Army," said Keith.

"I guess not," replied Ruth. "But he scared us with his talk."

"What if I told you that he wasn't lying to you? That he really is from the future."

"Oh, here we go again," said Bill. He got up to leave.

"Sit!" shouted Nicholas. "You called Pete a coward. Barbara was right, you're the coward. You're a coward because you're afraid to hear the truth. It might disrupt your comfortable little life."

Bill turned red again but didn't say anything. He sat back down.

"Pete was from the future," said Keith, "and so are we. And yes, Pete had responsibilities, but his responsibilities were in 2026, not 1917."

"I knew ... know Pete," said Barbara. "You've single-handedly destroyed his life—and all because you were afraid to confront something new. You should be ashamed of yourselves—both of you."

"We don't need to listen to this," began Bill, again standing up.

"Bill," said Keith quietly, "if you don't sit down, I will be forced to kill you. I've killed before and won't hesitate to do it again."

The blood drained from Bill's face, and he slowly sat down.

"As I said before, we are in a difficult situation. 'Desperate situation' is more accurate. Like Pete, we come from the year 2026. How we got here is too complicated to explain. But suffice to say that it was an accident. None of us wants to be here. I have a wife I love very much and who I might never see again because of this. Alice and Barbara—and Pete—are graduate students at Harvard. I don't know much about Nicholas—"

"The less you know, the better," said Nicholas.

"Okay," finished Keith. Nicholas's comment made him lose his train of thought. *What did he mean by that?*

He continued, "I could show you all kinds of things from our time, including this." He pulled a phone from his pocket and turned it on. He showed them the screen. Bill and Ruth jumped up and took a few steps back.

"This is a phone. It's nothing like telephones you're accustomed to. With this, I can talk to anyone else who has one—which is most people—from anywhere in the world. For example, I could call Alice or Barbara. And I can carry it with me wherever I go. You can sit down. It doesn't bite."

They slowly sat. Bill was clearly terrified of it, but Ruth exhibited a little courage.

"Do it," she said, "show us."

"I can't here. They need certain technology to work, and you don't have it here. All I can do is turn it on and show you what it looks like. I can take pictures with it, too."

He pointed it at Ruth and took a picture, then showed it to both of them.

Bill almost fell out of his chair, trying to back up. Ruth sat quietly and looked carefully at the picture, running her finger across the smooth surface of the phone.

"Oh, my goodness. You're telling the truth?"

"We are."

"Ruth!" shouted Bill. "You don't believe this drivel, do you?"

"Yes, Bill. I do."

Bill looked at Keith with suspicion.

"The boy—"

"Pete," said Barbara.

"Okay. Pete had a different name for the Great War. What was it?"

"World War One," they all said in unison.

Bill's mouth hung open.

"You said you've killed before," said Ruth. "Why?"

"I was in a war, too, in Iraq. Although, I doubt if it was called Iraq in 1917."

"It was called Mesopotamia," said Nicholas.

"How did you know that?" asked Alice.

"I just know."

"Anyway," said Keith, "there were a lot of wars after this one: World War Two, Korea, Vietnam, Iraq, Afghanistan, to name a few."

Bill slowly shook his head. "So, this is all true?"

"It's all true," said Nicholas.

"Did you fight?" Bill asked Nicholas.

"I did."

Since Nicholas wasn't forthcoming with any other information, Keith moved on.

"I know this is all a lot to take in," he said, "but trust me, we're still trying to come to grips with it, too. It's not easy for any of us—us or you. By the way, yes, I have killed before, but that was war. I would never kill you. All I ask is that you let us stay here for a while—maybe for the winter. We can't pay you, since all our money is from a hundred years in the future. But we can help out around the place. Maybe we can even give you business tips from the future. What month is it?"

"December," said Ruth. "December 7th."

"Wow," said Keith.

"What?" asked Bill.

"December 7th, 1941 was a big day in history. It was our entrance into World War Two," said Keith. "The Japanese attacked Pearl Harbor in Hawaii. After that, we also got involved in the war in Europe."

"Too many wars," mumbled Bill.

"Amen," added Keith.

"Yes, you can stay here," said Ruth. "It's the least we can do after the way we treated your friend. I feel ashamed of how we treated him. But we were scared."

"I understand," said Keith. "We are, too, and so was he."

"I just have one question," said Ruth.

"Yes?" answered Keith.

"You two girls. Were you part of the circus?"

"No, why?" said Barbara.

"That tattoo on your neck and the thing in Alice's nose. You only see those things in a circus."

"Ah, we have much to tell you," said Barbara.

Chapter 11

The winter progressed slowly. As the days flipped by, they had to accept that their world had changed forever. Both publicly and privately, there were many moments of tears from the two women and Keith. Nicholas showed little emotion and often kept to himself.

They waited patiently for a message from Ray Burton, but nothing arrived.

"He did say that it could take months," said Keith to the others one night at dinner. "After all, Pete arrived a few months before us. We just have to wait."

The holidays were particularly hard. Ruth tried to make them special by putting up Christmas decorations, but it only made them feel lonelier.

"I wonder what our families are doing for Christmas," said Alice, as they sat at the table on Christmas Eve.

"It's not Christmas at home," replied Keith. "We arrived December 7th, so we've been here eighteen days. We left 2026 in August, so it's still summer back home. I'm trying to keep track of how long we've been traveling. I don't know if it will mean anything in the long run, but it gives me something to do."

Bill and Ruth finally accepted the situation and became quite pleasant. The few times they had visitors, they introduced Keith and the others as old family friends.

Nicholas, however, remained an enigma. While he did his share of the work and was communicative when need be, they knew nothing about him. Nicholas never talked about his life. After ten days, he moved into the empty bedroom for the privacy it offered. Keith was secretly relieved he didn't have to share a room with the man.

*****

Christmas Day was a breaking point for Keith. Alice and Barbara had each broken down numerous times since arriving, missing home, family, and, in Barbara's case, Pete. But they were always able to recover and move on, at least until the next time. Throughout, Keith was the steady hand, always there to comfort them. But on Christmas Day, it all changed for him.

Ruth had made a nice spread of ham and mashed potatoes, with pumpkin pie for dessert. Midway through the meal, Keith suddenly felt sick and began to shake. From out of nowhere, the tears came. He quickly left the table and retreated to his room. Alice and Barbara were stunned at how quickly it appeared.

"We should go up," said Barbara.

"I would wait," cautioned Ruth. "He's missing his wife. There's nothing either of you can do about that. He needs to work through it."

Barbara looked at Alice in surprise. That was the most profound thing Ruth had said in all the weeks they'd known her.

"The human heart is not something I'm well-versed in," Nicholas said, "but I have to agree with Ruth. He needs time to work it out."

In his bedroom, Keith was sitting on the floor in a dark corner, talking to his wife.

"I'm so sorry, Cyndi. You kept asking me not to do the

explorations, and I ignored your concerns. But who could have predicted this? It doesn't matter. What's done is done, and I don't think I'll ever see you again. Ray tried to give us some hope that we'd return home someday, but we both know it won't happen. I'm so, so sorry. I love you. I hope you'll be able to forgive me."

He talked to her a while longer, then lapsed into silence. At one point, he drifted off to sleep, but woke up with a nightmare. They were going through another portal, and this one brought them to the Jurassic period. He watched as a velociraptor tore Alice apart. In his dream, he screamed. He watched in horror as she reached out to him for help. But he couldn't help her.

Damn movies, he thought when he woke up. Then he wondered, was there a portal that led to the dinosaur age? Sleep came again. This time, he didn't have any nightmares, but it was a troubled sleep.

He didn't move from his spot against the wall for the rest of the day. That evening, Alice knocked softly and asked if he was okay.

"No, but I just need to be alone. Thank you, though."

After that, Keith moved to the bed, where he stayed through the next day. He could no longer sleep. His thoughts turned to what they were going to do next. Was there a way to get home? No, of course not. But Ray Burton and Natalie O'Brien made it, so it wasn't impossible.

Twice, he got up to use the bathroom, but both times, he retreated to his bedroom, where he kept the curtains closed for the darkness.

Two days after abruptly leaving during dinner, Keith finally appeared downstairs. He knew that he looked ragged, but he didn't care. The two women and Ruth and Bill were all sitting in the living room in front of a fire. Ruth was knitting, and Alice and Barbara were reading novels they had found on the bookshelf. Bill was dozing. Nicholas had chosen to retire to his bedroom.

They all looked up as Keith entered the room. Even Bill sensed Keith's presence and woke up.

"Hi," said Keith. "I'm so sorry for my breakdown. It came on so suddenly, I just didn't expect it."

"That's often how they come," said Barbara, "when you least expect it. I was wondering when it would hit you. You've been there for the two of us during our moments. It was just a matter of time."

"Well, it hit me. That's for sure."

"Are you okay?" asked Alice.

"I'm not okay, but I made it through. Maybe it'll hit again. I don't know. But for now, I have to try to move on."

He smiled at Ruth.

"You don't happen to have any ham left, do you?"

They all breathed sighs of relief.

Keith was back.

Chapter 12

In the middle of February, the message from Ray arrived.

Bill returned from a trip to the shed with the red container in his hand. Attached to the container was a waterproof bag.

They had just sat down to dinner when he set it on the table.

"Is this what you've been waiting for?"

Alice squealed in delight. Barbara said, "Thank God." Nicholas smiled, and Keith grabbed for it.

"That's it!"

"It's a new container," said Nicholas. "The other one was probably in bad shape after more than a hundred years under the rocks."

Keith opened the bag first and pulled out something electronic. It wasn't large and had the vague shape of a flower vase. He set it on the table and opened the container. He pulled out the pad and a few other papers. Ray's letter was much longer this time.

Keith read it aloud:

Hi Keith, Alice, Barbara, and Nicholas (I got your names from the news reports of your disappearance),

I'm sure you've come to grips with the knowledge that you landed in 1917, give or take a year. Hopefully, you didn't have to wait long for this message. I'm counting on you being there to receive this. Please let me know if you got it.

Portals are not an exact science. In most cases, there is a window of a few months to a year. That's why your friend Pete is not with you. If the portal is degrading, the window could be up to a couple of years. Yours is still strong, which means a smaller window. That's why when I send a message, I don't know how long it will take for you to see it. Yours shouldn't take more than a few months.

The item I have included with this note is called a Portal Finder. As the name implies, it will help you locate active portals and tell you where they lead—to which time period. Included are the instructions for its use, along with some tips on finding portals. The Portal Finder might help you get home. But don't get your hopes up. Getting home is a long, arduous journey with no guarantees of success. At the very least, it might get you to a more palatable time period.

If there is someone you want to write a note to, please include it in the bucket. I will get the note that you send me, but this is the last note I will send, as they are about to fill in the hole where the hotel stood (and which they demolished soon after you disappeared). Once they do that, my ability to communicate with you will be gone.

I will try to track you, and if possible, I will leave you a message if I think you are headed for a particular portal—but as I said before, don't get your hopes up. Just to let you know, the Mountain Vista Inn closed because, over a period of a few years, five people mysteriously disappeared. We have to assume that they went through the portal. If that was the case, they will all most likely arrive sometime in 1917 or 1918, so be on the lookout for stragglers suddenly appearing. I think all the disappearances were in the 1950s and 1960s, so they will stand out by their dress, not to mention their confusion. Be aware of that.

On a somber note, be prepared that you might not make it home. If you arrive somewhere comfortable and where you don't stand out, consider making it your home. It's tough to think like that, but I'm just trying to present the reality. And if some of you want to stay someplace, but others want to keep going, you'll have to make some hard decisions—especially where it relates to the possession of the Portal Finder.

Here are some tips that might be helpful in your time travel journey:

- Try not to panic. It will only make things worse.
- Use your common sense when interacting with people.
- DON'T tell anyone that you came through time. It's a sure way to end up in a loony bin—or worse.
- In all the time travel movies, the characters are told not to interfere with time because it can change history. Based on an experience we had, the jury is still out on that one. However, to be safe, try not to kill anyone or make a significant change that might affect history.
- If you can move to a different time period, you might want to. If you know your history, you'll remember that the Spanish flu pandemic began in early 1918 and lasted a couple of years. 25-50 million people worldwide died from it. Be careful.
- You have one Portal Finder for the four of you—five if you find your friend. Try to remain friends. It could turn into a disaster if you don't. Be patient with each other. Understand that you will have differences of opinion, but try to settle them before you regret it. I suggest one person be in charge of the Portal Finder.
- You have no money, so you will not eat or have a place to sleep until you have some. Wherever you end up, get a job, if only for a few weeks before you move on. Without money, you're helpless. But in all honesty, sometimes you have to do what's necessary to survive, even if that means robbing a bank or stealing food.

- Not all time periods are friendly. It might come in handy if you can each get your hands on a small pistol.

- Know where you're going. The Portal Finder will tell you. What clothes do they wear in that period? What is their manner of speech, etc? When you arrive someplace, finding clothes to match the period will be the essential first step.

- We have two friends who are still traveling. Alex and Hanna. Hanna was one of the original travelers from the Time Travel Project in the year 2105. She knows the most about time travel. I will let them know where you are. They can track you just as I can. At the moment, they are in 1903. Whether they access another portal is up to them (it's a long story), but I know they will try to find you if they can.

- Be aware: We were told—and discovered for ourselves—that many of the portals are dying. So, you may see a portal on the Portal Finder, but by the time you reach it, it might have died. If you see a portal to a time that looks advantageous, don't hesitate to travel to it.

- You might have to go through several portals to reach a time where you can all feel comfortable.

This list wasn't meant to scare you, but the more prepared you are, the more successful you'll be. It will still be overwhelming at times, but preparation will help.

Good luck in your travels. Believe it or not, it's not all bad. Natalie and I had some nice times together at some of our stops.

All the best,
Ray Burton

They sat in silence when Keith finished reading the letter. Finally, Alice began to cry. Barbara put her arm around her and told her it would be okay. Keith thought that Barbara was close to tears herself. Then again, so was he. Meanwhile, Nicholas was deep in thought and was examining the Portal Finder.

Keith saw Nicholas raise his eyebrows at something in the note. What part was it? He couldn't remember. But noticed that Nicholas seemed surprised by whatever it was.

"What did your friend mean about the Spanish flu?" asked Bill. "It's February of 1918 now."

"We dealt with our own pandemic, and it wasn't fun," said Keith. "But they developed ways to fight it. With the Spanish flu, they had no ammunition against it. It just ran its course. In the process, millions died. It was especially significant because your population now is nowhere near what it is in 2026."

"What should we do?" asked Ruth.

"Try to limit your contact with others. If you must go into town, don't go at the busiest times. I know that this Inn is your business, but you might want to consider closing for a couple of years."

"We can't do that," said Bill. "It's our livelihood."

"Maybe the pandemic wasn't as bad in the rural areas like New Hampshire," suggested Barbara.

"That's possible," said Keith. "The worst of it was probably in the cities. All I can suggest is that you be careful. If one of your guests looks ill, have them isolate."

They discussed Ray's message for a while longer, with the two women deciding to write to their parents the next day.

"Maybe your Christmas present was this contraption," said Ruth. "Maybe it will get you home."

"That's a nice thought," said Alice.

Nicholas set the Portal Finder on the table.

"Well?" asked Keith.

"It's quite simple," said Nicholas. "Ray's directions were clear. Like he said, it shows portals all over the world—both incoming and outgoing portals. The incoming ones won't be of any help, but the outgoing ones will. He says the closer you get to a portal, the more precise the Portal Finder is—down to feet and inches. He says it's essential to go through holding each other's hands. Otherwise, you won't end up together. That's what happened with Pete. And it's why we all arrived together."

"That was lucky that you suggested it," said Keith.

"Yes, lucky," said Nicholas.

There was something behind the way Nicholas said it, but Keith couldn't take the time to try to figure it out.

"What did you find with the portals?" he asked.

"Like it or not, we only have one choice. It's in Nebraska and takes us to the year 1950. All the other portals are out of the country."

"What about Pete?" asked Alice.

Silence descended on the room.

Finally, Nicholas said, "I don't see any way we can find Pete. There are a couple of portals in Europe, but this is not the time to go there. And they don't go to very advantageous times. It would be too dangerous, not to mention the obstacles we'd face just getting there."

"As much as I hate to say it," added Keith, "I'm afraid we've lost Pete. None of us wants to hear this, but he's in France—or on his way to France—fighting a war. If I remember my history, the conditions there were atrocious. Even if we somehow made it to Europe, we'd never find him. Not to be any more morbid than I've already been, but he might already be dead."

As Keith expected, that news didn't go over well with Pete's two friends. They hugged each other and cried. To his surprise, Ruth was also crying.

"It's all our fault," she said. "If we hadn't been so cruel to him, he might still be here."

"Please don't blame yourself," said Keith. "This hasn't been easy for any of us. It's all so hard to believe."

"Maybe," said Bill gruffly, "but we could have been kinder."

"What's done is done," said Nicholas. "We need to make plans."

"I guess we are going to Nebraska," said Keith.

Chapter 13

NORTH CONWAY, NEW HAMPSHIRE—2026

I held the note from Keith.

> *Hi Ray,*
>
> *We got your note in February 1918, two months after we arrived. Thank you for the Portal Finder and all the good suggestions.*
>
> *Enclosed are notes from Alice and Barbara to their parents. They also wrote one to Pete's parents. Nothing from Nicholas to anyone. I've also included a letter to my beloved Cyndi.*
>
> *Sadly, we have to come to grips with the fact that we've lost Pete. He was forced to join the Army and we must assume he is now in France, fighting that terrible war. There's nothing we can do for him. We have to move on.*
>
> *The only portal that makes sense to access is in Nebraska and leads to 1950. You can tell your friends, Alex and Hanna, in case they can find us. We'll see where we go from there. One thing at a time. If it's feasible, we'll try to find a spot near the portal to leave you a message. Maybe you'll be able to locate the portal.*
>
> *If you ever want to look them up, the people we are staying with are Ruth and Bill Hobbs, the original owners of the Mountain Vista Inn. Before we read your caution note, we had already told them where we were from. Unfortunately, we had to tell them—we had no choice. They now believe us and have been good to us.*

We can't think of anything else to tell you. We are all scared but thinking clearly. Hopefully, we will make it home. But if not, maybe we'll find a good place to settle.

Thank you for everything!
Keith

I hoped my tips would be helpful. Most were common sense, but from my experience in that situation, sometimes common sense was hard to find. And I was older and had spent a lifetime in rough situations. Most of them were young. Their nightmare was only beginning. I couldn't help thinking that none of them would survive the ordeal, which made me sad.

I also felt sorry for their friend, Pete. There was no one he could go to for help. He was stuck there and would never leave. All I could hope was that he was able to adapt. But again, I doubted it—especially since he was going into the bowels of that war.

I would let Alex and Hanna know about this group in my next communication with them. According to Alex, they were becoming bored where they were and were thinking about accessing a portal again. That would be risky for Hanna, as she had already experienced mild Portal Sickness. A severe case could be deadly if she went through another portal.

Well, that was their decision. We all had our own decisions to make with time travel. They'd make the one that was right for them.

*****

As expected, I received both responses from Keith on the same day I sent mine. After all, their messages were well hidden in the rocks under the bridge for over a hundred years, whereas mine had to deal with the vagaries of time travel. I also knew from experience that their second reply wouldn't appear until after I sent the message to which they were replying. It made sense—one of the only things about time travel that did.

I stayed that night in a hotel. I called Natalie, and we talked for a while, but she was exhausted from her day, so I called it a night and got to bed early. I took one last drive out to the site the next morning.

It was good that I warned Keith that it would be my last communication with them because the workers arrived that day—on a Saturday, no less—and filled in the hole.

That was a portal that would never be used again.

I was anxious to get home and was on my way after checking for one final note from them. But there was nothing. I stopped in downtown North Conway for a sandwich. While I sat in my car eating it, I booked a flight from Boston to Toronto the following afternoon. I'd spend a few days with Natalie, then fly to Quebec City, where a portal existed. It was the latest one that I was using to communicate with Alex and Hanna. At a later date, I would also fly to North Dakota and put the same message in the portal there. It sounded like they might be headed in that direction next. When I got home, I would send the notes to the parents of Alice, Barbara, and Pete. None of them lived anywhere close. I had no idea what the reception to the notes would be, but that wasn't my problem. I would also give Cyndi the note from Keith in person before I left for the airport. She deserved to hear as soon as possible.

As I thought about the possible reactions from the parents of Alice, Barbara, and Pete and the teary reception I was undoubtedly going to get from Cyndi, I began to think that this wasn't my path. I could research with the best of them and write like there's no tomorrow—an interesting saying, considering the subject matter—but I didn't deal well with real-time human emotions. I could already guess the kids' parents would think it was all a hoax. Did I really want to have to explain myself? It was time to get Natalie's input on it all.

I arrived home after midnight. I should've been tired, but I wasn't. I had started thinking on the trip home about Keith and the others. It was Nicholas that I was curious about. Why did he have no one to contact?

So I spent the next hour online, trying to find information on him. Nothing. Nothing at all. That was curious. Everyone has a footprint online, even if it's a tiny one. But there was nothing for Nicholas. That was usually indicative of someone who lived off the grid. It could also mean something else.

That "something else" was confirmed the next morning by a visit from Hal and Simone.

Seeing them was always a treat, but this time, they entered my house with serious expressions.

"This doesn't bode well," I said as I let them in.

"It doesn't," said Hal. "And unfortunately, I don't think there's anything that we can do about it."

I grabbed bottles of water from the fridge, and we all sat in the living room.

"I had a note sitting on my desk," began Hal, "with the names you gave me of the people who went through the North Conway portal. When Simone came in and saw the list, I thought she was going to faint."

He nodded for Simone to take over.

"Have you found any information on Nicholas Gates?" she asked.

Why did I know it was headed in this direction?

"No, at least not *that* Nicholas Gates. I was looking him up last night and was puzzled by it. I began to wonder if maybe he was a time traveler. I'm guessing I was right?"

"It's more than that," she said. "Much more."

"Uh-oh."

"Uh-oh is right," said Simone. "Your time travelers are in great danger."

Chapter 14

"When I saw his name on the list," said Simone, "my whole body froze. And then I thought that it had to be a coincidence. After all, it's not an uncommon name. But the more I thought about it, the less I thought of it as a coincidence. How many people with that exact name could be involved with time travel? So, we needed to come by to confirm it with you."

"And to scare me."

"There's always that added bonus," said Hal, chuckling.

A little bit of humor went a long way. After all, it wasn't something that affected us directly, and there was nothing we could do to help the others.

"In 2104, the year before we all left as part of the Time Travel Project," began Simone, "a major event dominated the news for weeks—maybe months. Over thirty members of a humanitarian organization were killed in their New York offices. Someone went in and slaughtered them all. No one survived. Two people weren't in that day, but the person who slaughtered the workers in the office found them and killed them at home. In an instant, the organization ceased to exist."

"And the killer was Nicholas Gates," I said matter-of-factly.

"It was. As for why he did it, no one knew. All he said publicly when he was caught was that they were dangerous to the world and had to die. They were the ravings of a lunatic."

"I'm guessing he escaped?" I asked. "Since you are intimating that this Nicholas Gates and your Nicholas Gates are the same person."

"He did. He was somehow familiar with our project. He broke into our offices, stole a Portal Finder, and accessed the portal in the basement of our building. That took him back to 2010, or so. I assume he found another portal or two after that."

"I noticed that one of the travelers had a stronger residue than the others. It must have been him," I said. "I took a picture of it and was going to show you."

"You don't have any pictures of Gates, do you?" asked Simone.

"No. Cyndi saw the group before they left. She said he was an older guy in his fifties—"

"I resent that," said Hal. "Older guy?"

"I resent it too," I said. "I'm there myself. Anyway, she said he was tall and thin and looked his age."

"Sounds like the same man," said Simone.

"Then you're saying that Keith, Alice, and Barbara are traveling with a mass murderer."

"Sounds like it."

"And now there's no way to contact them."

"I'm not so worried about Keith and the others," said Hal. "But if he's that deranged, what damage can he do as he travels? I know we haven't proven one way or the other that you can change history, but still, if it's possible, he could do a lot of bad stuff."

There was nothing more to say, so Hal offered to take me to the airport. I told him I needed to stop at Cyndi's first, and they were happy to accompany me.

We arrived at Cyndi's, and she met us halfway up the walk to the front door.

"Any news?" she asked, giving Hal and Simone the once-over.

"Cyndi, this is Hal March. He was a fellow traveler. And this is Meriam Smith," I hesitated, "who is kind of an expert on time travel."

"You don't have to cover for me with Cyndi," said Simone. "My name is Simone, and I'm a time traveler, too," she said, shaking Cyndi's hand.

Hal and I gaped at her comment.

"I'm tired of hiding," she explained to us. "And Cyndi deserves full disclosure." To Cyndi, she said, "I'm a scientist. I come from a time in the future, and I've done a lot of research on the subject—not to mention a lot of traveling."

I couldn't believe it. Simone might not have been healed from her horrible experience in the 1700s, but to make herself known was a significant step.

Cyndi led us inside, and we sat in the living room. "Do you have news?"

"I do," I said. "But not the news you want to hear. I also have a letter for you from Keith. I haven't read it. Before you read it, let me apprise you of the situation."

Cyndi nodded her head dumbly, not wanting to hear what I had to say.

"Keith and the others landed in December of 1917. They were going to stay with the owners of the Mountain Vista Inn until spring, when they would head to Nebraska to find a portal that would take them to 1950."

"How do they know about the portal?" she asked.

"I provided them with a gadget to help them find portals."

From the corner of my eye, I saw Simone jerk and Hal close his eyes. Did I miss something?

"I was going to tell you," I said to them. "I assumed you'd approve."

"No, that's fine," said Hal.

But it wasn't fine. Something was going on that they hadn't told me. I'd have to wait until we left to find out what it was.

"So, they can find their way home?"

"This is the part you don't want to hear," I said. "Cyndi, even with the gadget, the chances of them finding their way home are slim at best. Luck played as much a part in our returning home as anything did. For them to find a portal that would bring them back even close to now is a stretch. I don't know what Keith wrote in his letter, but I'm guessing he will probably tell you to get on with your life and not wait for him."

Tears were rolling down her cheeks. She ripped open the envelope and started reading silently. When she finished, she broke down. Simone sat next to her and hugged her without saying a word. Finally, Cyndi composed herself.

"Yes, that's pretty much what Keith said. I won't tell you the rest because it was personal, but he doesn't think they will make it back. You people and your time travel."

"Cyndi, we didn't invent the portals. They are a fluke of nature."

"I know. I'm sorry. That wasn't fair."

We stayed with her a while longer. Simone gave her Hal's phone number and told her to call if she ever wanted to talk. Cyndi said she would—that there were things she wanted to understand.

When we were back in the car and Hal was driving to the airport, I said, "Okay, what did I do wrong when I gave Keith the Portal Finder?"

Simone motioned for Hal to tell me.

"I know your intentions were good," Hal said, "but you may have just made their situation even worse!"

Chapter 15

I looked to Hal to finish his explanation.

He, in turn, looked over at Simone with an expression I couldn't read.

"What?" I asked. "You didn't want me to give them the Portal Finder?"

"Normally, I wouldn't mind," said Hal. "Hell, you know that. I trust your judgment completely."

"Then what do you mean by 'normally'?"

Hal looked at Simone again. This time, he seemed to be looking for guidance. I suddenly felt a rock in the pit of my stomach. What was I missing?

Simone let Hal off the hook.

"You know that I've been studying portals, trying to figure out what makes them tick and why so many of them are dying," she said.

"I do."

"I've been tracking them using the Portal Finder we keep in the safe. Hal taught me how to use your archaic spreadsheets."

"She keeps calling them that," said Hal.

"In 2105, we had much more advanced ways of tracking information. Anyway, I've been tracking the portals for months. Last week, I had to revisit some information, only to find it wrong."

"Wrong in what way?"

"The portal I looked at supposedly went to the year 1816. But when I checked the 1816 portal, it didn't exist."

"But we already knew that portals were dying," I said.

"Dying, yes. But not shifting. There seems to be a total upheaval with the portals. When a portal dies, it disappears from the portal finder. Obviously, when it dies on one end, it also dies on the other. You can't have a portal that leads nowhere. But what I discovered is scary. When I found the discrepancy with the 1816 portal, I checked a few more. Ray, about half of them were wrong!"

"I'm not sure I understand. Wrong in what way?"

"Using the 1816 portal as an example, I went about it in reverse—which was no easy task, I might add—and discovered that the portal emptied out in 1924, not 1816. But the Portal Finder still showed it as 1816."

I felt a shiver run up my spine.

"Over the past week, I've checked almost a dozen more. Only half of them went where the Portal Finder indicated. The others had wildly diverse results, with the target portals being anywhere from 10 years to 175 years different from what the Portal Finder showed. And upon checking a couple of the shifting ones again, the target date had changed a second time."

"How can that be?" I asked.

"Who knows?" answered Simone. "I haven't had time to search for an explanation yet. I've been too busy looking for the anomalies. All I can tell you is that the portals are shifting somehow. There must be an explanation, but I can't tell you what it is."

"The Portal Finder was correct in showing where Keith and the others are," I said.

"And that would be among the fifty percent that are

accurate," said Simone. "I can't tell you more than that because I haven't yet figured it out. I'm not sure I will figure it out."

"So, it's possible that I might have sent Keith and the others to their deaths."

"You don't know that," said Simone. "You've seen as many travelers as I have. They don't tend to live long lives. We were the lucky ones. Natalie and Alex went through portals by accident and survived. Natalie's companion, Randy, didn't. You and Hal knew where you were going and made it okay. I knew where I was going and almost died. What's the term you use, Hal? Crapshoot?"

Hal nodded.

"It's a crapshoot," said Simone. "There are so many factors involved, but it often comes back to the strength of the person who accesses the portal. I guess what I'm saying is that they might go through a portal thinking they are going to one place and end up in another. But in the end, it might not matter—it might all end up being how well the traveler can deal with it."

"I need to let Alex and Hanna know," I said.

"I'll write up my findings so you can pass it on to them," said Simone. "I'll email them to you."

"Thank you. Then I'll print them. Let's hope I can get it to them before they decide to travel somewhere."

I caught the 5:00 flight to Toronto, anxious to see Natalie, but suddenly feeling stressed.

Had I made a big mistake deciding to research potential travelers?

Chapter 16

"I keep getting the nightmares, Ray, and I don't know what to do about them."

Shooting had finished for the day. We were in Natalie's palatial hotel suite, lying in bed, with Natalie's head on my chest and her shoulder-length brown hair covering my chest. Due to flight delays, I didn't arrive until midnight the night before. Natalie needed her sleep for the next day's shoot, so we didn't have time to talk. It was now the next day, and we were anxious to spend some quality time together.

"It's not like I can see a shrink," she continued. "They know nothing about time travel."

"But they know about traumatic events," I countered. "Whether it's time travel or losing a loved one, it's still trauma."

"And that's the problem," she said, "it's both. I've been having dreams about Randy, the guy I came through the portal with."

"Wow, I had almost forgotten about him," I said.

"Me, too, and maybe that's why I'm dreaming about him. Maybe it's guilt. I wasn't in love with him, but I cared about him. And when I found out that Max killed him, it affected me. But why did I so quickly forget about him?"

"Well, you kind of had a lot going on."

She gave a sad smile.

"That was while it was all happening. But now I should be reflecting on it all, but instead, I'm making movies."

"You are reflecting, but it's coming as nightmares. You think you should somehow feel guilty, but there's nothing to feel guilty about. Just yesterday, Simone talked about the strength of the traveler. Some people can handle it, and others can't. In fact, she mentioned Randy as an example. Going through that portal was an accident, and you both dealt with it differently. Focusing on your movies is exactly what you should be doing now."

"You're right, but it doesn't solve the problem."

Natalie had gone through the Hollow Rock portal with her boyfriend, Randy Brown. While both were terrified at what had happened, Natalie did her best to accept the situation. Randy went the other way, becoming less and less stable and making dangerous comments about time travel to the populace of Hollow Rock. The town Marshall, Max Hawkins, also one of the original travelers in the Time Travel Project, had seen enough from Randy. After giving him every chance to stop his wild behavior, Max finally took Randy to the desert and killed him.

Randy was the first of Natalie's losses. She developed a close relationship with Beryl Dixon, a famous mystery author from the 1930s who had also gone through the portal. When Beryl died, Natalie sank into a deep depression until I showed up and helped her escape that life.

"Natalie, we lost people during the years we were traveling, people we had grown fond of. It's to be expected that the effects of it would hit us."

"It hasn't hit you," she said.

"It has, but in a different way. You have to remember that we have different life experiences. You grew up in a tough neighborhood but then moved to Hollywood and fell into that life. You're tough, but you haven't seen what I've seen. In my years as a journalist, I covered some of the worst situations imaginable and lost a lot of people I met and cared about. That prepared me—as much as anything could—for what we went through."

I kissed her on the top of her head.

"You said you feel it in a different way," said Natalie. "In what way?"

I was quiet for a minute. This was Natalie's time for sharing, not mine. I told her so.

"I have more to tell you," she said, "but I want to hear what you're going through. You've said you're lost, and I agree with you. Talk to me about it."

"You have your career," I said, "Hal has the book, and Simone has a whole new life to learn. I was already finished with my career before I went through the portal. I had moved on to writing fluff pieces. The assignments were crap, but it was a comfortable life."

"So you were kind of lost even then," said Natalie.

"I guess I was."

"Coming after me gave your life purpose."

"It did. I thought researching missing people would also give me purpose, but it hasn't. It's not what I want to be doing."

"I've known it for a while," she said. "I was trying to give you the space to get through it. I knew your research project would land you in the same place, but you had to find that out yourself."

"We know what my problem is, and I've just got to figure it out. So, let's get back to you. What do you think started the nightmares?"

"I know exactly what started them. I haven't told you yet, but I got an email from Randy's brother. I don't know how he got my email address. Anyway, he threatened me—not explicitly, but the intent was clear. He says that he doesn't believe his brother is dead. He says that I abandoned Randy. He wants proof that Randy is dead. He said we don't have it."

"Proof? His bones are probably somewhere under the sand, and wherever it was that Max killed him probably has a condo complex on top of it by now. Did you answer him?"

"I shouldn't have, but I did. He made me feel guilty. I told him I felt bad that he doesn't have closure, but there is no way to provide him with proof."

"Don't respond anymore."

"I won't. But you don't understand. This is why I'm getting nightmares. He wrote back."

"And?"

"He says he knew I couldn't prove it because he has proof that Randy is still alive!"

Chapter 17

"What? That's ridiculous," I said. "He's just trying to get the publicity—or money, more likely."

"Probably, but there's no way Randy could still be alive, is there?"

"I wasn't there, but you said that Max told you he shot Randy in self-defense, and he fell off a butte, right?"

"That's what Max said," replied Natalie, "but I never believed the self-defense part of the story. I know Max took him out to the desert to get rid of him. Randy was getting out of control. I never forgave Max for what he did, but at the same time, I understood why he felt he had to do it."

"What kind of person was Randy?" I asked.

"He was fun at first. I think he wanted the relationship to be more than it was. It never would have been. He wasn't the 'long-term' kind of relationship person. But he was the only person I told that I was retiring from acting. Huge mistake. We had already kind of broken up when he suggested our infamous hike in the mountains around Hollow Rock. I never should have agreed to it. That's when I realized he was partly with me for my fame. A 'hanger-on,' so to speak. Still, his death came as a shock."

"Didn't someone find the body?"

"I don't remember. I think someone ran across some remains

at one point, but it could have been anyone who had died in the desert. No, there is no way Randy could have survived. He would have come back to town."

"Unless he knew that coming back would get him killed for real," I said. "No, he's dead. He has to be. His brother sounds like a carbon copy of Randy—in it for the money."

I kissed her again.

"Stop with the nightmares. Randy wasn't your fault or your responsibility. And as for the others who died, what can I say? Everybody dies. Just some sooner than others. Enjoy the fact that we did the improbable. We made it back after being lost in time."

"You're right. I'll keep thinking good thoughts and double up on my sleeping pills."

We both laughed at that.

"Now all we have to do is find something you can grab onto," said Natalie.

"I'll find something. Meanwhile, I'm going to find Randy's brother and put a stop to this."

"How?"

"He'll either show me proof of Randy's existence or agree to leave you alone for good."

I didn't need to explain it any further.

Natalie had a strenuous work schedule coming up, so two days later, I left for Quebec City to leave the messages about the portals and Keith and the others for Alex and Hanna. Simone had emailed the explanation to me, and I printed copies for the two portals where I'd be leaving it. I waited a day near the Quebec City portal—a hole in the ground in a lonely patch of woods a few miles outside the city. There was no response from Alex and Hanna. The next day, I headed for Florida.

*****

As hard as it was to believe, when we returned from our journey through time, my condo in West Palm Beach was still there and still in my name. It gave me a place to stay while I checked out Sammy Brown, Randy's brother, who lived down the road in Fort Lauderdale.

Before leaving for my adventure through time, I had my accountant take over the condo fees and insurance payments. There was enough in the account to take care of it (and pay my accountant) for several years, even though I wasn't sure I'd ever make it home. When I returned, I decided to keep the place as a getaway for us. This would be only the second night I'd slept in it since returning. It brought back many old memories, which, of course, paled in comparison to the new memories.

I liked that Natalie was back doing something she loved, but I did miss her. We had spent much of the last few years inseparable, so at times like these, when I was in my condo all alone, I really missed her.

I called her that night, and we talked for an hour. I think she sensed my loneliness, but I could tell she was exhausted, so I let her go to bed, promising to let her know what happened with Randy's brother.

The following day, I drove to Fort Lauderdale. Sammy Brown lived in a modest neighborhood in the shadow of the Hard Rock Guitar Hotel, an enormous structure shaped like a guitar that could be seen from miles around. Sammy's house was on a dead-end street with only two other houses. There was a ten-year-old Jeep in the driveway.

I'd barely finished knocking when the door opened. The man on the other side of the cheap screen door looked like a homeless person. His long blonde hair streaked with gray was full of knots, and he had a few days' growth of beard. His eyes, though, were clear.

"Ray Burton. I wondered when I'd hear from you."

"Sammy Brown?" I asked.

"Very observant of you. Come in."

I didn't like him. He had an obvious chip on his shoulder, with an attitude to match. He tried to look dangerous, but it was all a charade. I had dealt with many dangerous people in my life, and this guy didn't hold a candle to them.

The living room was surprisingly light and clean—the opposite of what his appearance displayed. We moved to the kitchen, and he motioned for me to sit on one of the hard kitchen chairs. It's funny how many people prefer talking in the kitchen. Or maybe he was sending me a message that I didn't rate the living room.

"My comment about Randy caught your attention?"

"I'm here for one reason only," I replied. "Mostly to warn you never to contact Natalie again, or I will make sure you regret it for the rest of your life."

"That bitch." He said it under his breath, but I was meant to hear it.

I jumped out of the chair so fast it tumbled behind me. He leaped from his chair, not expecting my reaction. I grabbed him by the throat and pushed him against the wall.

"Wait … wait … wait," said Sammy with a gurgle. "I'm sorry."

I let up a bit, but just a little bit.

"Seriously, I'm sorry." He was having trouble breathing. "I was just going by Randy's comments. He didn't think very highly of Natalie O'Brien, or should I say Natalie Fox?"

I stopped in mid-choke. Nobody knew that name. Nobody. We had never mentioned it in any interviews. It was the name Natalie took when she was stuck in Hollow Rock.

"How…?"

"How did I know it?"

"Yes."

"Randy told me. Can you let go of my neck now?"

I released him and returned to my chair, which I had knocked over. I put it back in place and sat.

"Talk."

He rubbed his neck. "In news reports and interviews with Natalie, she said that she came through the portal with Randy, but that he was later killed. She's never gone into detail about that."

"Because it was nobody's business," I said.

"It was our business—his family's business—to know, and she never once contacted us."

"An oversight on her part that she regrets. You will never understand the things she went through, both in Hollow Rock and after, and many of them were better forgotten. And with all the time travel deniers out there, we all felt it better to keep low profiles—or, in her case, as much of one as she can. So, contacting the family of a friend who'd been killed wasn't high on her list. Understandable, especially since you've been stalking her."

"I haven't been stalking her!" He said it louder than necessary. "I just want the truth."

"You have a strange way of getting there."

"You're right. I'm sorry."

"Okay, here's the truth. I never met your brother. I arrived a few months after Natalie. But here's what I know after talking to her and others who were there when he was. Going through a time portal, especially when you go through it accidentally, is a shock to the system. Natalie and Randy went from 2009 to 1870 in an instant. You can only imagine what it was like. I've been through a number of portals, but they were always my choice, and it still took a lot of getting used to.

"It was tough for Natalie, but she kept her wits about her. I know you don't want to hear this, but Randy was the opposite. He couldn't handle it. He went off the deep end. He began telling the townspeople that he was from the future. He had been explicitly told by a seasoned time traveler never to reveal that information, but Randy was out of control. Natalie began to distance herself from Randy, which didn't sit well with him. Finally, Max, the town marshal, and a time traveler, rode with him out to the desert and shot him. Max claimed that Randy attacked him, but Natalie knew better. She knew that Max killed Randy to shut him up. She avoided Max after that. Max said that after Randy was shot, he fell off a butte. Now you're telling me that Randy lived?"

"He was found by some Indians, who nursed him back to health," said Sammy, rubbing his neck. "He was with them for months before leaving."

"And you know this how?"

"He wrote us a letter."

Chapter 18

Was this for real?

I was about to find out.

Sammy stood up and went to a desk, where he picked up some papers.

"This is a copy of his letter," he said. "I have the original in a safe deposit box. My parents live on a farm in Arizona. It's been in my family for generations. There's a well on the property that was used in the early days. Of course, they've had running water for decades, but the well still exists. Randy knew the well had survived, so he put a letter in it, hoping that one of us would find it someday. Two months ago, my father was cleaning out the well and found the note. It was sealed in a very old liquor bottle—a message in a bottle, so to speak."

He handed me the letter. I was almost afraid to read it. How would Natalie feel if she learned that Randy lived?

Dear Mom, Dad, and Sammy,

I don't know how long I will have been gone by the time you get this, but please know that this is real. As hard as it might be to believe it, I went through a time portal that brought me to the year 1870. I was with Natalie when we discovered a cave near the ghost town of Hollow Rock near Flagstaff. It brought us to the actual live town of Hollow Rock—a bustling town of about 200 people.

In the weeks that followed, Natalie abandoned me for the town marshal, named Max Hawkins, who was an experienced time traveler. Max took me into the desert and shot me. He thought he had killed me, and he pushed me over the side of a hill.

I was found by a band of Indians, who nursed me back to health, and I stayed with them for a few months. When I was healthy, I left and found my way to Tucson, where I got a job at the newspaper. I've been in Tucson ever since.

That was thirty years ago. I'm now sixty years old and still healthy. I learned from Max (before he "killed" me) that time travel is a fluid thing, so when you get this, I might have been gone a day, a year, or twenty years. I just don't know.

I don't know what happened to Natalie, the bitch. She had changed her name from Natalie O'Brien to Natalie Fox. Max told her that it was necessary to do that. I kept my name and am proud of it. I will never forgive her for abandoning me like she did. I was struggling to adjust, and she just cast me aside. A few years after arriving in Tucson, I met an old Hollow Rock resident who told me that Natalie met another guy, and they went to San Francisco. I don't know what happened after that.

Please know that I miss you all! I've often returned to the cave that brought us to 1870, but I was told that portals are only one way. So, I know that I'll never go home again. My life has turned out okay. At the newspaper, I worked my way up to assistant editor. Occasionally, I write a story and make a veiled reference to you or to the 21st century (a word here or there that might spark something). You can probably find issues from 1890 to now, 1902, online. Look for articles written by me.

Also, please know that time travel is real. I wish it weren't, but it is. I often wonder how many people have gone through portals and are stuck in time. Max once told me that there were hundreds of portals.

Now, at least, you can put to rest the question of why I suddenly disappeared.

I love you all!
Randy

There was no doubt that this was authentic. He wrote it in 1902. That was the time period Alex and Hanna were in. I wondered if it would be worth asking them to see if he was still there. It would give them a mission. And it might also give Sammy a chance to send his brother a message for some closure.

"I have some friends traveling in 1903 right now—or whatever 'right now' means in the scheme of things. If you want to write a note to your brother, I can send it to them."

"Seriously?"

"Seriously. I doubt if they can get him home, but I'm sure they will try. But something you need to know. Natalie didn't abandon Randy. He made it impossible for her to remain with him. His behavior had become erratic. I went through the same portal as Randy, but I did it on purpose. I'm the one who took Natalie to San Francisco. We met up with Max, who was later killed in an air raid in London in 1942."

"Good."

"And Natalie isn't a bitch. She's a wonderful woman with a kind heart."

"I'm sorry I called her that. I guess I didn't know the full story."

"I haven't even touched on the full story. My friend, Hal March, is writing our story. He'll get into it in much more detail. And now I can let him know about Randy. It would be nice to add that."

"Thank you."

The chip on his shoulder was gone. He truly appreciated my offer.

"I'll give you time to write something. I'll be in West Palm Beach one more night, then I'll stop by tomorrow morning for your letter. If you could make a couple of copies and some copies of Randy's letter, that would help. I leave messages for my friends in a few spots, just in case. This way, they will get it no matter where they are."

We shook hands, and he apologized several more times for his email to Natalie and for calling her a bitch.

That night, I called Natalie and told her of my visit.

"I can't believe he lived through that," she said.

"You're not going to start feeling guilty again, are you?"

"No. What you said was right. He brought it on himself. What Max did was wrong, but I had no control over that. So, no, I won't feel guilty any longer. Changing the subject, I imagine you're going to the portals to leave Alex and Hanna the messages?"

"I am. I tried Quebec City and didn't get a response. It would have come in immediately. They hinted in their last message that they might find a portal. They seem bored with the early 1900s. I left them the information on Keith and the others in Quebec City, but now I have to visit that spot again, as well as the other spots to let them know about Randy. But first, I'll try the portal in North Dakota—they may have returned to the States. And maybe they haven't accessed another portal yet."

"I don't blame them for wanting to move on. It seems like a boring time in American history—but I'm not well-versed in history."

"This coming from a time traveler," I said, laughing. "Heck, you've lived more history than most historians have researched."

"I guess that's true. I worry about Hanna, though. If she goes through any more portals, she might die of Portal Sickness."

"That's one of the reasons I'm going to pass on Sammy's note to them. Maybe it will give them the incentive to stay in that period and not risk her health."

The next day, I was on my way to North Dakota. If they got my message, it would be up to them if they wanted to pursue the mission. My guess was that they would.

After all, as Alex could attest, Hanna was a sucker for lost time travelers.

Chapter 19

NORTH DAKOTA — 1903

"Are you sure?" asked Alex. "I don't have to tell you how dangerous it might be for you."

"You don't," Hanna replied. "But you also don't have to tell me that if we stay here any longer, I will go out of my mind. You will, too. You just don't want to admit it."

"I agree," said Alex, "It really sucks to be stuck in a time period that you can't relate to. But again, do you want to risk your health?"

Alex and Hanna were trudging down a dirt road on their way to the portal they had used once before to communicate with Ray and the others. Since last using this incoming portal, they had been from one end of Canada to the other and were now back in the States. While the pristine beauty of the Canadian wilderness had been breathtaking, it was time to move on. There was a portal in Nebraska that led to 1950, and after accessing that one, according to the newer Portal Finder they were using, one on Cape Cod that emptied out in 2030.

"There's no guarantee I'll get sick again," Hanna said.

"But there's nothing to say that you won't get sick," countered Alex.

When Eliminators sent to kill the time travelers began dying of a strange illness, Alex, Hanna, and the others discovered that it was caused by too much travel through portals. Most of the Eliminators had accessed numerous portals. Hanna, the most experienced traveler of the group, caught a mild case of Portal Sickness and was told by Fletch, a scientist who had traveled back in time, that more traveling could result in a fatal case of Portal Sickness.

"It's just two more portals," said Hanna, "and then we will be reunited with Simone and the others. I sometimes wonder if we should have gone with them when we had the chance."

"Putting aside the fact that it would be dangerous for you, it was something neither of us wanted. The technology of the era would be far more advanced than anything I had known in the 1970s, and not advanced enough for you, from the 22nd century."

"And at the time," said Hanna, "it seemed the right thing to do. Now, having suffered through the mentality of the early 1900s, it's much more appealing."

"It is. But—"

"But you're scared for my health. I get it, and I appreciate it, but I've made up my mind. We'll see if there's anything from Ray at this portal, then head for Nebraska."

"Another hotbed of 1903 sophistication," said Alex. "And don't think I can't see through you. With a goal of 2030, if you end up dying, at least I'll be among friends."

Hanna gave him a wink.

"I'd rather be with a 'live' you alone, than a 'dead' you and be with the others," said Alex. "But I respect your decision."

That seemed to put the discussion to bed, and they walked a while in silence. An hour later, they reached the portal, located in the crack of a cliff.

"We've got mail," said Hanna, spying a gray container in the portal. They used a gray container to blend in with the color of the rocks around the portal.

As Hanna opened the container, Alex scouted the area to

ensure they were alone. When he returned, he asked, "Good news or bad?"

"Mostly bad," answered Hanna. "You can read it, but the gist is that Simone has discovered that portals are suddenly depositing people in times different from what the Portal Finder indicates. She says it's about a fifty percent chance of being sent someplace other than your intended destination."

"Well, that's not good. It makes us rethink our plans."

"It does. Want to go on a rescue mission instead?"

"Oh?"

Hanna passed on the information about Randy in Tucson.

"Ray included a copy of the letter he sent to his brother. Based on what Natalie said, I thought Max Hawkins killed Randy, but I guess not. If we're willing, Ray would like us to go talk to him and determine if he wants to try to go home, or, at the very least, give us a message to pass on to his family."

"Sure, why not? It's not like we're under any deadline. And the longer I can keep you out of a portal, the better. Anything else?"

"Yes, a mass murderer from my time escaped. He's now part of a group that accidentally went through a portal in New Hampshire in 2026. Ray has been in touch with them but didn't know about the mass murderer until it was too late."

"That's scary," said Alex. "But at least it doesn't affect us."

"We hope," said Hanna. "I remember the reports. This guy was bad."

They left a message for Ray that they'd try to find Randy, then informed him that they would try for a portal to take them to 1950, and then another from there to 2030.

"If they work, look for us in 2030. If they don't, this will probably be the last you'll hear from us. Love to you all!" Alex and Hanna

Minutes later, they were back on the dirt road, on their way to Tucson.

Chapter 20

Using a series of trains and a lot of walking, Alex and Hanna finally made it to Tucson.

As they approached Tucson on the Southern Pacific train, a man in the seat across the aisle from them pointed out the window.

"That's where it happened."

"Where what happened?" asked Alex.

"The Esmond Train Wreck."

"I've heard about that," said Alex.

As a former history teacher, Alex observed places from a new perspective as he traveled through time.

"What happened?" asked Hanna.

"You ain't heard about it?" asked the man. "Two trains ran into each other head-on. Fourteen people died. It only happened a few months ago. I thought everyone had heard of it."

"I don't get out much," said Hanna, smiling.

The train had arrived too late in the afternoon to look up Randy, so they checked into a hotel and had a leisurely meal.

As Hanna slept that night, Alex was wide awake. Accidentally accessing a portal in the 1970s that led him back to the 1920s was a traumatic event, as was almost being killed by an Eliminator. But then Hanna appeared on the scene and saved him.

They were about the same age—just past forty—but the lines in Hanna's face and her wisps of gray hair made her appear older. It was the stress of many years of solitary time travel, accessing more than two dozen portals. Alex hadn't looked in a mirror lately. Was he showing the same signs of stress? He was almost afraid to look. It didn't matter. He knew the answer—of course he was.

Yet despite her ragged appearance, Hanna was still beautiful—both inside and out. Taking in the splendor of the Canadian mountains had calmed them both down, but it wasn't enough—they needed to settle down someplace that made them happy and content. Would they ever find the peace they were looking for?

Sometime in the middle of the night, exhaustion took over, and Alex finally fell asleep.

The next morning after breakfast, they got directions to the *Arizona Daily Star*. Randy said he worked in a newspaper, and the *Daily Star* was the largest. They could work themselves down to the smaller papers from there if that wasn't the right one.

As it turned out, they picked the right newspaper, just not the right time.

"Hi, we're looking for Randy Brown," Alex said to the receptionist.

"Oh, you're looking for Randy? Oh, uh, let me get someone for you."

She quickly got up and vanished into the newsroom.

"Hmm," said Hanna. "That's an interesting response."

"Sure is."

After five minutes, an older man entered the room with the receptionist.

"It's these two," she said.

The man shooed her away and sat on the edge of the desk. He looked the part of a newspaper person, with an ink-stained white apron and a visor. He was in his late fifties or early sixties, bald with wisps of white hair. He wore horned-rim glasses.

"I'm Joseph Mattson, the publisher. Excuse the apron, but I was helping to fix an issue in the printing department. You're looking for Randy Brown?"

"We are," said Hanna. "Is there a problem?"

"As a matter of fact, yes. Are you related to him?"

"No, but we're good friends with his brother. We promised him we'd stop in and say hi to Randy."

"Your name wouldn't be Natalie, would it?"

"No, I'm Hanna, and this is Alex, why?"

Instead of answering the question, he said, "I'm afraid Randy is in a spot of trouble. He's under arrest."

"Oh no," said Alex. "What did he do?"

"You're familiar with the Esmond Train Wreck?"

"Of course," said Alex. "Randy didn't have anything to do with it, did he?"

"No ... well, we don't think so. The problem is that Randy seemed to know about it before it happened."

"How could that be?" asked Hanna innocently.

"We don't know. Randy has been a good employee for a long time. A little strange at times, but that's the newspaper business—we attract them. But a few days before the crash, he started warning people about the impending crash. How he got that information, we have no idea. When questioned, he refused to speak at first, then he came up with a story of being from the future. That's when he started talking about this Natalie person and how it was all her fault. The police couldn't make anything of it, so they put him in the local asylum. So, he is technically under arrest but getting mental help."

Knowing what Simone went through in a French asylum in the 1700s, Hanna seriously doubted that Randy was getting "help."

"Do you know anything that could clear it up?" asked Mattson.

"No," said Alex, "but we'd love to talk to him. Maybe we can get him to explain himself. Even though he doesn't know us, maybe mentioning his brother would help."

"The police station is across the street," said Mattson. "I'll walk you over there and introduce you to the sheriff."

Alex and Hanna glanced at each other, concerned that this situation was about to take a wrong turn. However, they followed Mattson across the dirt street. It had rained briefly, which kept the dust down.

The sheriff—Hayes was his name—was a no-nonsense sort, but intelligent.

"Hey," he said, "if you can get him to talk and tell us how he knew about the accident, I'd be forever in your debt."

"Forever?" asked Alex, liking the man.

Hayes smiled. "Temporarily."

"We'll see what we can do," said Hanna.

The sheriff sent for a taxi for Alex and Hanna—a horse and buggy—and rode his own horse to the asylum. After paving the way for their visit, the sheriff wished them luck, then left.

"That was risky of the sheriff, leaving us here alone with Randy," said Alex.

"I think the place freaks him out," said Hanna. "He was sweating by the time he left."

The head of the asylum had an orderly take them to Randy. Being officially under arrest, he was in a locked room by himself. The orderly unlocked the door and held it open for them.

"Want me to stay?" he asked.

He seemed happy when Alex told him that he could leave, that they'd be fine.

"I'll be nearby if you need any help. Randy's a nice guy."

Randy was lying on the bed, reading a book. As they entered, he set the book down, removed his reading glasses, and examined his two visitors.

"You don't look like cops or doctors, so who are you?"

Randy was tall and thin, with longish gray hair that covered the tops of his ears. His expression was one of suspicion.

"My name is Alex, and this is Hanna. We have a letter to give you from your brother."

"You what?"

"Sammy wrote you a letter. We haven't read it, of course. It was passed onto us by a man named Ray Burton from 2026."

"No shit?" He sat up straight.

"We also came here to ask you if you'd like to try to get home, but your current situation makes that rather difficult," said Hanna.

Randy shook his head. "What exactly is going on? Are you travelers?"

"We are," said Hanna. "We traveled with Ray Burton, who talked to your brother, and Natalie O'Brien, who you know."

Randy's face changed at the name being mentioned.

"And before you go off on a tirade about Natalie," began Alex, "what happened to you was your own fault. We talked to others who were there when you arrived in Hollow Rock." That wasn't true, but Alex figured Randy wouldn't know that.

"They said you were reckless and constantly said things about time travel that you were asked not to. Max Hawkins didn't want to shoot you. He just had no choice in his mind. As far as Natalie is concerned, it was your idea to go into the cave, not hers. And she distanced herself from you because of your actions. But she had no idea what Max was going to do. So get off the Natalie kick."

"Natalie is a good friend," said Hanna. "And she doesn't deserve your hate. You're blaming her because you don't want to take responsibility for your actions. So, before we go on, do you understand what we're saying?"

Randy held up his hand to stop her.

"I get it. I've always gotten it. I just haven't wanted to accept it. It was easier to blame her than to admit my stupidity. How did you know about my Natalie tirades, though?"

"The letter you sent to your family."

"In the well?"

"Yes, Ray said something about a well. It was also things you said to the sheriff," said Alex.

"Can I see the letter from my brother?"

"Yes," said Hanna. "But our question to you is, do you want to go home? We can't guarantee we'll make it, but it's the best chance you'll ever have."

"I do."

"Then, while you're reading the letter, Alex and I need to figure out how to get you out of here."

Chapter 21

"What do you think?" whispered Alex.

The room was small, so there was no privacy to discuss the situation. Luckily, Randy seemed engrossed in his brother's letter.

"The best idea is to try and convince the sheriff that Randy dreamt the whole thing and is a little off-kilter. We can tell him we'll bring him back to his family for support."

"And if it doesn't work?"

"We need to get him out of here," answered Hanna, "we have no choice. We can't have him spreading the word that he's a time traveler. We have weapons. We might have to use them."

They each carried a weapon from the 22nd century. Alex thought they resembled the phasers from the Star Trek TV show. Like the Star Trek phasers, they could be set on stun or kill. What made these especially unique was the ability to do a group stun — to stun anyone within a six-foot radius. The only problem with the group stun was the longevity of the effects. An individual stun could knock a person out for an hour or so, whereas the group stun would only be good for a few minutes.

"But let's take it one step at a time," continued Hanna. "We'll try the sheriff first. If that doesn't work, we … what's the word you use?"

"We punt," said Alex.

"Right. We punt. I have no idea what that means."

"I'll explain it later."

Randy had just finished his brother's letter and was lying on the bed crying. Alex and Hanna gave him time to compose himself. Finally, the tears ended. Randy looked up at them from the bed, his eyes red-rimmed, and said, "I want to go home."

"We'll talk to the sheriff and see if he will release you to our care."

"And if he doesn't?"

"We'll punt," said Hanna, flashing Alex a smirk.

"We'll get you out of here," said Alex. "Just be patient."

"Understand," said Hanna, "we can't guarantee anything. We can see a way to get to 2030, four years from when your brother wrote the letter. But portals have been dying, and we've just found out that those that are active are now only fifty percent accurate."

"Look," said Randy, "I'm in my sixties and I've kind of burned my bridges here. I honestly don't know what came over me to mention the Esmond Train Wreck. Maybe I knew that people would die and I thought I could prevent it. Anyway, I'm tired of living. If I can make it home, it might rejuvenate me. If not, I feel I'm reaching the end. I made do with a bad situation as best I could. But look around you. Is this the era in which you would want to spend the rest of your life?"

"Not at all," said Hanna. "It's something Alex and I were discussing recently."

"Then you know why I'll take the chance. At this point, I have nothing to lose."

"Okay, hang in there," said Alex. "We'll be back."

Randy stood up and gave each of them a hug.

"Thank you."

Once outside, Hanna said, "That's a very different Randy than Natalie described."

"He's also thirty years older," countered Alex. "It sounds like life has worn him down. He also told his brother that life was good for him, but that's obviously not true."

"If he had just kept his mouth shut, this would be easy," said Hanna.

"It was his mouth that got him in trouble the first time," said Alex. "I guess there are some things you don't learn with age."

They walked the mile from the asylum to the jail. The sheriff was sitting behind his desk when they walked in. With the times in mind and the prejudices against women, it was decided that Alex would do most of the talking.

"What's the verdict?" the sheriff asked.

"He's a loon," said Alex. "The whole thing about the train was a dream he had, but I think it was enough to push him over the edge. Because of the dream, he started to believe that he had traveled through time."

"So you think we should keep him in the asylum?" asked the sheriff.

"Ultimately, it's your decision, but if I could suggest, I think he would benefit from living with his family back east. Keeping him in the asylum would be a waste of the taxpayer's money."

"While I agree with you about the waste of taxpayer's money, I can't just let him go. He might be sick in the head, but he might also be lying to you about the train. No one has a dream like that before the event. I don't know how, but he's somehow connected to the wreck."

"It was an accident, wasn't it?" asked Alex, trying to remember the vague story he had once read about.

"Maybe. A train operator never delivered the message for one of the trains to go onto a side track. The operator admitted that he never sent the message."

"So he was at fault," said Alex.

"Yes, but why didn't he?" asked the sheriff. "That's the question that was never answered. The operator disappeared the next day. Pretty suspicious. I've always wondered if it was done on purpose. If that's the case, then your boy in the asylum knows something he's not telling us. Until he does, he's staying right there."

After saying goodbye to the sheriff, they walked slowly back to the hotel.

"Well, it seemed like an easy enough job—go down to Tucson and ask someone if he wants to go home," said Alex. "Who would have thought we'd run into this?"

Deep in thought, Hanna didn't say anything. Alex watched her for a minute, then stopped and grabbed her hand.

"I know what you're thinking. You're wondering if we should kill him. Do we have the right to do it?"

"I'm considering it. There was a time when I would have said that we definitely have the right," answered Hanna. "At the time, the secrecy of the Time Travel Project was at stake. But there isn't a Time Travel Project anymore. And even if there were, I wouldn't care. Eliminating Randy would be the simple solution. After all, he's already in a mental hospital."

"But?"

"But I've spent too much time hanging around with you. You've instilled in me some morals that I had lost."

"You never lost them. You had a job to do, and it wasn't a pleasant one. You didn't have a choice."

"We always have a choice," replied Hanna. "You taught me that. I look at Randy and wonder what would give me the right to end his life. This poor guy has been living a nightmare for the last thirty years. We have the means to get him home—well, maybe—so he can catch up on lost time with his family. Shouldn't we try to give him that opportunity?"

"So, what's the plan?" asked Alex.

"I have no idea."

She looked at Alex with determination.

"But we have to break him out."

Chapter 22

That afternoon, they sat in a park and considered their limited options.

"Getting him out of the asylum will be easy," said Hanna. "What we do after that is not so simple. We can't get lost someplace. The only viable means of escape is the train, but we can't just take him out of the asylum and hop on the train. Only a couple come through a day. And we have the sheriff to deal with."

"Maybe it will just have to do with timing," suggested Alex. "We buy three tickets on the next train. One of us gets Randy while the other stuns the sheriff and locks him in a jail cell. He probably has a bunch of deputies, so if they are there with him, we stun them, too. Then we hop on the train."

"Kind of shaky," said Hanna.

"I agree."

The park in which they were sitting was near the train station. They watched as a westbound train pulled into the station. A few minutes later, it chugged off.

"Busy time of day," said Alex. "The eastbound train was only here an hour ago."

They looked at each other.

"That's it!" said Hanna. "If we time it so it all happens before the eastbound train arrives, the sheriff will assume we went east.

Randy's brother lives in the east. So, what if we hid for an hour and took the westbound train?"

"And you can buy three tickets for the eastbound," said Alex, "and I'll buy two for the westbound. When they switch ticket agents, I'll buy a single ticket for the westbound. They'll remember you buying the three tickets, but not me buying two and then one. They'll assume we went east.

"The sheriff will telegraph the police at all the eastbound stops. By then, we'll be someplace west—maybe Los Angeles. From there, we can take a more northerly route and then go east to Nebraska."

"It might just work," said Hanna.

*****

That afternoon, Alex bought a ticket for the next day's 2:30 westbound train. The next morning, Hanna bought three tickets for the 1:00 eastbound train, and a few minutes later, Alex bought two tickets for the westbound train, making sure it was a different ticket agent from the previous afternoon.

At 11:00, Hanna entered the front door of the asylum and stunned the receptionist before she was aware of Hanna's presence. Sneaking through the corridors, she was able to avoid being seen. When she arrived at Randy's corridor, she hit the attendant with a blast from the weapon, pulled him into a broom closet, and stole his keys.

When Hanna reached Randy's room, she unlocked the door and said, "Move. We have to be quick about this."

Randy didn't hesitate. He jumped up and followed Hanna from the room. No other words were spoken. Hanna closed and locked the door behind them, then returned to the attendant and attached the keys to his belt. She then closed the closet door.

They managed to leave the asylum without being seen and

then walked toward town.

"No one saw us," said Hanna, "so hopefully, they won't immediately notice that you are missing. By the time they do, we should be long gone."

"I can't thank you enough for coming for me," said Randy. "For the first time in thirty years, I have something to look forward to."

"Let's just hope Alex is doing as well," said Hanna.

He wasn't.

At that moment, Alex was sitting in a jail cell, with a deputy pointing his gun in Alex's general direction and nervously pacing back and forth. He held Alex's weapon in his other hand with two fingers as if it might explode.

It had started well. Alex saw through the window of the police station that the sheriff had his back to the door, going through paperwork. Alex quietly opened the door and stunned the sheriff. The sheriff collapsed, and Alex dragged him to one of the cells. As he closed the cell door, he heard the front door open.

"Sheriff, you back there?"

It sounded like it might be one of his deputies.

As the man entered the jail area, Alex hit him with a stun blast before the man saw him.

It was as he dragged the deputy into the cell with the sheriff that his luck ended.

"Don't move. Don't you move. Drop whatever you have in your hand, or I will shoot you, godammit."

Another deputy had walked in without Alex hearing him.

Alex dropped his weapon.

"What did you do to the sheriff?" he asked.

"The sheriff is fine," answered Alex. "He'll wake up in a bit. Nobody is hurt."

"Get into that cell, or you will be."

Alex entered the cell next to the one with the sleeping men, then the deputy closed and locked the door.

As he paced back and forth, he was fearfully eying the weapon in his fingers.

"I'd be careful with that," said Alex. "It's dangerous."

"Don't tell me what to do," the man said nervously. He set the weapon on a table next to the door. "What is it?"

"It's dangerous."

"I heard you. What is it?"

"Better that you don't know."

"By golly, you better tell—"

He dropped to the floor.

"I'm always saving your butt," said Hanna, stepping into the jail area.

"And I appreciate it," said Alex. "I almost made it without anyone seeing me. He showed up while I was dragging the other deputy into the cell."

Randy got the deputy's keys and unlocked the door, then he and Alex pulled the deputy into the cell.

"He's the only one who saw me, but we've never seen him before, so he doesn't know who I am."

Hanna looked at the clock. "It's 1:00. The train arrived early, so it should be leaving momentarily. We need a good hiding place for the next hour or so."

"How about right here," suggested Alex. "We can stay back here by the cells. If someone comes into the office and doesn't see the sheriff, they'll probably leave. If they come back here, we stun them. Meanwhile, if the sheriff wakes up, we stun him again. That should give us the time we need."

"Great idea," said Hanna.

During the next hour, they had to stun each of their prisoners one more time, and only one person entered the office from the street. Through a crack in the door, Hanna saw that it was a man in a white uniform. He called for the sheriff, but getting no response, he hurried out.

"I think it was someone from the asylum," said Hanna. "That means they've discovered you missing," she told Randy. "When we go to the train station, we should all get on separately. We can sit together when we get on, but I think it best not to be seen together in the station."

The plan worked without incident, and an hour later, they were on their way to Los Angeles.

Three days later, taking a roundabout route, they disembarked the train in Fremont, Nebraska. Using the Portal Finder, Hanna found the portal that would take them to 1950. It was at the bottom of a crack in the ground on a boulder-strewn hill. The portal was about thirty feet from the surface.

"Not exactly easy to get to," said Alex.

"But it's a crack in the rock, not dirt," said Hanna, "so the chances are good that we won't be buried alive when we go through."

"That could happen?" asked Randy.

"Anything can happen," replied Hanna. "I once went through a portal and found myself underwater. A lake had appeared in the intervening years that covered the portal in water. It was a shock, but luckily, it wasn't too deep. But it's a real fear. We could get there and be buried under twenty feet of dirt. But as I said, this is rock, so we're probably good."

"Probably?" asked Randy.

Hanna just shrugged.

"There's no sense in hanging around here," she said. "The sooner we go through the portal, the better."

"Our first step toward getting to 2030," said Alex.

"Let's hope it takes us there," said Hanna. To Randy, she said, "We have to hold hands going through, or we might not end up together."

"Whatever you say," said Randy. "I'm just grateful to be gone from Tucson."

"Speaking of which," said Alex, "how did you know about the Esmond Train Wreck? It's not exactly a well-known piece of history."

"I grew up in Arizona. I also spent some time in Tucson after college, interning at the *Arizona Daily Star*. It was just one of those things I learned."

"Wait a minute," said Alex. "You worked at the *Daily Star* in the late 1800s until we got you, and you also worked there in …"

"In 2002, just for a short time."

"That should set some kind of record," said Alex.

They all laughed.

They began their climb down into the crack.

"Stop when you reach the bottom," said Hanna. "The portal is only five feet away, near that overhang."

A few minutes later, they were all safely at the bottom.

Hanna said, "Are we ready?"

"Not as much as I was before you gave the scenario of coming out thirty feet underground, but I guess so," said Randy.

Alex just looked at Hanna and crossed his fingers. She knew what he was thinking.

She kissed him and said, "I'll be fine. Don't worry."

And then they stepped through.

Chapter 23

FREMONT, NEBRASKA—1950

"How do you feel?"

They hadn't been out of the portal for more than thirty seconds when Alex was quizzing Hanna.

"Alex, I'm okay. Besides, if I'm going to get Portal Sickness, it won't happen instantly."

They were still at the bottom of the chasm, which looked almost the same as in 1903, except now there were dozens of empty liquor bottles.

"Looks like it's a popular place to party," said Randy. "Probably a teenage hangout."

"Looks like they party at the top and throw their garbage down into the crevasse," said Alex.

They climbed to the top and looked around. A wire fence had been placed around the area of the hole, but a portion had been cut and opened for the partygoers. Not much else had changed, though. They could see the town of Fremont a couple of miles away. In all other directions was farmland.

Hanna checked the date on the Portal Finder.

"April 3rd, 1950. Well, this one was accurate. Let's hope we get just as lucky with the next one."

"Chilly out here," said Randy.

Hanna and Alex dug out sweatshirts from their backpacks. Alex had an extra one and handed it to Randy.

"You're taller than me, but it might fit," said Alex.

"I'm sure it'll be fine. Thank you."

They started walking the dirt road that led to Fremont.

"Where is the next one," asked Randy.

"Cape Cod," answered Hanna.

"A bit of a distance from here," said Randy. "I went there once. It was summertime and crowded. The roads were congested."

"My family had a summer house there," said Alex.

He stopped dead in his tracks.

"Holy shit! It was the 1950s when we went during the summer. My house is probably there right now."

"You had a summer house?" asked Randy. "You're from the 50s?"

"Actually, I was born in 1935 in New York. The portal I went through was in 1973. It took me back to the 1920s. I come from a rich family. My parents eventually disowned me because I wouldn't join the family business. My parents were typical rich snobs. Even though Cape Cod was a vacation spot, I never felt like I was on vacation when I was with them."

"That sounds miserable," said Randy.

"It was. The good news is that Cape Cod in the 1950s isn't crowded. Hanna, where on the Cape is the portal?"

She looked at the map.

"Somewhere near the town of Falmouth. It's called Woods Hole."

"Ha! That's where our summer home was—or, I guess, where our summer home *is*. Nobody will be there yet this early in the season, so maybe we can check it out."

"The portal is right on the coast near the water," said Hanna.

"Hopefully, it's accessible."

They walked silently for a few minutes, and then Randy asked Hanna, "So, what's your story?"

"I'm from the 22nd century. I was born in 2082, so I guess I spent much of my early life in the 21st century, but I was part of the Time Travel Project. I left there in 2105 with five others to learn as much as we could about time travel and report back our results. I think we all came to the same conclusion that it shouldn't be played with."

"Why? Because you can change history?"

"Well, we're not sure that's the case," said Alex. "I had an experience in Australia with my grandfather, who was killed right in front of me, but it didn't seem to change anything. I still have memories of him from when I was growing up. We think it's impossible to wipe out experiences that have already happened."

"But to answer your question," added Hanna, "it's more a case of the physical and emotional toll it takes on the traveler."

"I can relate to that," said Randy.

"Exactly. Of the six of us who left in 2105, only two of us are still alive—me and a woman named Simone. Max Hawkins, who shot you, was one of us. He died in an air raid in London in 1942."

"Good. He got what he deserved."

"Max wasn't a bad person—none of us were—but we all had to do things against our nature. Shooting you was definitely extreme, but we all took our jobs seriously. It was felt that those who accessed portals by accident were better off dead than to suffer the anguish of being lost in time. Someone back in my time even had the bright idea of sending back assassins—they called them Eliminators—to do that job. We think they are all dead now. What I'm trying to say is that there are aspects to all this that you can't understand."

"And some aspects that I can."

"Exactly."

When they arrived in Fremont, they headed straight to the train station, only to find out the next train east wasn't until the following day. The ticket agent directed them to a hotel in the center of town, but only after staring at their strange combinations of old clothes with modern sweatshirts.

"I think it's time to buy some 1950s-appropriate clothes," said Alex.

They stopped in a clothing store and bought a couple of outfits each.

"It's a good thing Josef gave us so much money when we left Seattle," said Hanna.

"Who's Josef?" asked Randy.

"Another accidental traveler," said Alex, "but one who struck it rich in the Yukon gold rush. He made sure we had enough to keep us going. Which reminds me, we should send Fletch and Josef a letter before we cross over to a new time to let them know what we're doing."

"We'll write it tonight, and we can send it in the morning," said Hanna.

As they left the store and headed for the hotel, Alex said, "Wow."

"Wow, what?" asked Hanna.

"I'm looking at the stores. This is the time of my childhood. In 1950, I was fifteen. Although most stores were mom-and-pop stores like so many of these, there are some chains that bring back memories—Woolworths over there, and Western Auto," he said, pointing across the street. "Even though we lived in a swanky part of New York City, we sometimes took road trips to small towns. That was the best time I had with my parents."

Alex had taken on a reflective look, so the others remained silent.

They were about to cross Main Street when Hanna suddenly said, "Oh. My. God."

"What?" asked Alex.

"I'd know that face anywhere," said Hanna. She looked in her backpack for her weapon. "There's someone who needs to die."

PART TWO

Chapter 24

NORTH CONWAY, NEW HAMPSHIRE—MARCH 1918

A month had passed since getting Ray's final note. Life with Ruth and Bill was comfortable but boring. The couple lacked the sophistication that Keith and the others were used to a hundred years in the future. Their whole existence seemed to revolve around daily tasks. When things were slow in the evenings, there were many occasions where Keith attempted to question them about their beliefs and goals, but he was met with confusion.

While anxious to check out the portal in Nebraska, it was still winter, and traveling there would be difficult.

"It doesn't matter when we arrive," said Nicholas. "Time is fluid. We could go through the portal now and land in September of that year, or we could go through it five months from now and arrive in May."

"So you're saying that we shouldn't be in a rush to get there," said Keith.

"Exactly. We'll get there when we get there."

"How do you know this?" asked Keith.

There was a slight hesitation. Very slight, but Keith caught it.

"I've listened to some of the interviews with Ray Burton and Natalie O'Brien."

It was a good save, but Keith wasn't convinced. There was more to Nicholas than met the eye. He had felt that from the beginning.

Ruth and Bill occasionally traveled into North Conway for supplies. Keith wasn't worried about them revealing the presence of the travelers, as they had all become quite close. Sometimes, Alice and Barbara accompanied the brother and sister into town. Alice had taken out her nose ring, and Barbara made sure to cover her tattoo. Keith, being at the upper age of soldiers sent overseas, elected to stay at the Inn. The more he stayed out of sight, the better. Otherwise, it would raise too many questions. As an older man, Nicholas could have gone into town without raising undue interest, but he was not inclined to do so and elected to stay at the Inn.

The subject of Pete was never brought up when the group got together. Ruth and Bill were wracked with guilt about it and preferred to forget it ever happened, and Keith and Nicholas had only known Pete for a few hours before he disappeared.

However, it was a different story when the girls were behind closed doors. Barbara brought him up whenever she and Alice were alone. Alice quickly realized that the relationship between Barbara and Pete was deeper than they had let on.

"Alice, I miss Pete," Barbara said one night. It was her usual way to begin the conversation.

"I know you do. I do, too, but obviously not in the same way you do. You bring him up every night. It seems to be eating you alive, and I don't know what I can do."

"You can't do anything, but I can," replied Barbara. "We had ... have ...something special, and I don't know if I can go on without him."

"What are you saying?" asked Alice, fearing that Barbara was talking about suicide.

"Have you seen the posters in town for the ambulance

corps?" asked Barbara.

"I've seen them but didn't really read them."

"They are looking for women to become ambulance drivers overseas."

"Do you mean overseas in the war?" asked Alice with a shocked expression.

"Exactly. I remember reading something about that at school. Women played an important role in the war. And this might give me a chance to find Pete."

Alice was shaking her head as Barbara talked.

"No. That's a stupid idea. Think about it, Barbara. The chances of you finding Pete are miniscule. You don't know where you'd be stationed or where he is. You could both be over there and never meet. Pete might already be dead."

"Don't say that."

"I will say it because you're not being realistic. You have no idea where Pete is, and he has no idea where you are. He doesn't even know that you came through the portal. In his mind, he's all alone."

"Which is why I have to find him," said Barbara. "And maybe I can help while I'm there."

"Help who? The past has already happened. The First World War came and went over a hundred years ago. Some people died, and some lived—you won't change that. Come with us to Nebraska and go through the portal. Maybe we'll find a way home."

"You don't really believe that, do you? We're never making it home. The sooner you accept that, the better. We'd have to find all the right portals. It can't be done. Even Ray Burton said it was unlikely."

"But not impossible."

Barbara sighed. "No, not impossible. But extremely improbable. Alice, you have to move on. Hook up with Keith.

Have some kind of life."

"Hook up with Keith? Barbara, he's married."

Barbara saw Alice's flushed expression and smiled.

"C'mon, Alice. I've seen the way you look at him. He's smart, good-looking, and seems to understand the situation. Most of all, he needs you. He may not know it yet, but he does. He was married in 2026. In 1918, he's a single guy. Ask him if he believes we'll make it home. If he's honest with you, the answer will be no."

"I notice you haven't asked me to go with you," said Alice.

"It's not your path," replied Barbara. "Yours is to try to find your way home. It won't happen, of course, but in the process, you might find a life with Keith. Just watch yourself around Nicholas. I don't know what it is, but he's not who he says he is. It won't matter, though. I don't think he'll stick with you guys. Just watch that he doesn't steal the Portal Finder."

"It sounds like you've made up your mind," said Alice.

"I have."

"Will you do me a favor and at least think about it overnight?" asked Alice, hugging her.

"I will."

When Alice woke up the next morning, Barbara was gone. On her pillow was a note:

I thought about it.
I love you! I'll miss you!
Have a great life.

Chapter 25

"What do you mean she left?" asked Keith the next morning.

Alice told Keith at the breakfast table. It was just the two of them. Bill and Ruth were outside doing chores, and Nicholas hadn't come downstairs yet.

"She must have walked to town last night. She's joining the ambulance corps. She wants a chance to find Pete. We talked about it for a long time last night. She said she would think about staying, but that was just to appease me. She had no intention of staying. She also said that if you were being honest, you would admit to me that we'll never make it home. She also said to watch that Nicholas doesn't steal the Portal Finder. She's suspicious of him."

"Yeah, I haven't figured him out yet, either."

"So?"

"So what?"

"Are you going to be honest with me?"

Keith looked down at his food, then pushed the plate away.

"No, I don't think we'll make it home."

He had tears in his eyes. Alice put her hand on his.

"Thank you for being honest."

Keith put his other hand on hers.

"I'm sorry," he said.

"For what?"

"For putting all of us in this situation."

"It wasn't your fault. How could you have known?"

"Still…"

Alice took a deep breath. Was she ready to tell him this? She never would have said anything if Barbara had stayed. But now, Keith was all she had left.

"Barbara said something else."

"What?"

Alice took her hands back and sat with her arms crossed. She looked down at the floor, not wanting to see Keith's expression when she said it.

"She said I'm in love with you. She said she could tell because of how I looked at you. She said we're going to need each other. I said you were married, and she said you were married in 2026, not 1918, and that it didn't matter because we were never going home."

Alice realized what she had just said.

"I'm sorry."

Tears were flowing down her face. She jumped up and ran up the stairs to her bedroom, shutting the door behind her. She flopped onto her bed and sobbed into her pillow. Had she just ruined everything? Keith was the only friend she had left, and now she had just put a wedge between them. She just told him that he'd never see his wife again. Oh, why did she listen to Barbara?

About fifteen minutes later, a knock came softly at her door. The door opened, and Keith stepped in.

"Can we talk?" he asked.

Alice nodded, sitting up and wiping away tears.

Keith came over and sat next to her on the bed. He took her hand.

"I'm deeply in love with my wife," he began.

"I'm sorry," said Alice. "I didn't mean—"

"Please let me finish," said Keith. "What you said hit me hard."

"I'm s—"

Keith held up a finger, and Alice went silent.

"It hit me hard because as much as I know it to be true, I've refused to accept it. I've always imagined seeing Cyndi again. It will only be through a miracle that I'll ever see or even communicate with her again. That's hard to accept, especially since it hasn't even been four months. But while it's four months since I saw her, it's over a hundred years away. Barbara was right. We'll go to the portal in Nebraska. That will take us to 1950. Then what? Where will the next portal take us? It's a puzzle. We have to fill in the pieces. We know what the finished product should look like, but getting there is the problem. I'm sorry, I'm rambling."

He squeezed her hand.

"Barbara was right. We will part ways with Nicholas at some point, and it will just be you and me. I find you attractive, and I like you a lot. I haven't gone beyond that because of my loyalty to Cyndi. But it's time to accept the reality of the situation. Since meeting Cyndi, I've never been with another woman, so you'll have to give me some time to work it through. But Barbara was right—we will need each other."

He kissed her lightly on the lips.

"From this point on, it's you and me."

Chapter 26

A week after Barbara left, they were sitting down to dinner when Bill entered the kitchen out of breath.

"Bill, what's wrong?" asked Ruth with concern.

"Someone … someone near the shed." He was trying to catch his breath. "I think one of yours."

Keith realized what he was trying to say. Someone had just accessed the portal. He jumped up and ran for the door. Nicholas and Alice were right behind him. They arrived outside to find an older, heavyset man standing outside the shed, looking around him with eyes as big as saucers. He jumped when he saw Keith and the others.

"Who … what … what happened?"

"It's okay, sir," said Keith as he reached the man. He spoke quietly so as not to panic the man more than he already was.

"I don't understand. I don't understand." The man looked to be on the verge of tears.

He was obviously a kitchen worker. From his clothes, Keith deduced that he was probably a dishwasher. He looked to be close to seventy, with gray short-cropped hair, and very overweight.

Keith tried to calm the man, who was driving himself into a panic attack.

"So cold … snow … how? It's summer." He grabbed Keith's shirt. "It's summer! What's happened? I don't understand. Who are you?"

"Calm down, sir, and I will try to explain it to you."

"I don't understand. I don't understand. This isn't supposed to be here."

"Come inside with us. It's warm in there, and we can explain what has happened to you."

"No. No! I don't know you! Get away from me!"

He pushed Keith away and tried to run through the snow to get away from Keith and the others. But the snow was two feet deep, and the man was exerting all his energy but making little headway. Suddenly, he froze mid-step and fell face forward into the snow.

Keith reached him and rolled him over on his back with the help of Nicholas and Alice. Keith felt for a pulse.

"No pulse."

He began CPR on the man while Alice continued to feel for a pulse.

"Nothing," she said after a couple of minutes.

Keith continued for a minute longer, then stopped.

"I'd guess he had a heart attack," he said.

"Probably better that way," said Nicholas.

"What do you mean?" asked Alice.

"Look how panicked he was. There was no explanation you could give him that would calm him down. He was probably a simple man with a simple view of life. He would never have survived. This way, it was quick and simple."

Bill and Ruth had put on coats and joined them. Keith gave them a quick explanation.

"We'll have to call Doc Billings," said Ruth. "Where should we put this man?"

"How about the mudroom?" suggested Bill. "It won't be in the Inn, but also won't be outside."

"Good idea," said Keith.

With Keith and Alice lifting the man's legs, and Nicholas and

Bill lifting his shoulders, they half-dragged and half-carried the man back to the building. It took them almost a half hour to get him into the mudroom. Meanwhile, Ruth called the doctor, who said he would be out in an hour or so. He didn't see the need to rush, seeing as the man was dead.

"Check his pockets," said Nicholas. "He shouldn't have anything on him from that era. He should have nothing on him but his clothes."

As it turned out, the man had no identification of any kind, as well as no money.

"He must have changed into this outfit at work," said Keith. "That's good."

Doc Billings arrived about an hour later, along with Sheriff Kush and a truck to transport the body. Doc Billings was a self-important little man whom Keith and the others immediately disliked. It may also have been the knowledge that he was responsible for Pete's disappearance.

They brought two bruisers, who loaded the man onto the truck.

"Who was he?" asked Kush—another one they took a dislike to.

"Don't know," said Bill. "He just appeared behind the house. We have no idea how he got there."

Sheriff Kush looked at Keith. "Why aren't you overseas?"

"None of your damn business," said Keith. He wasn't going to give the sheriff the satisfaction of an answer.

"He had polio as a child," said Bill quickly.

Sheriff Kush stared at Keith, then turned and strode out of the Inn.

"You don't want him as an enemy," said Bill.

"He doesn't want me as an enemy," said Keith.

"Or me," added Nicholas.

Keith stared at the retreating sheriff, then said to Bill and

Ruth, "You might have others come out of the portal. Ray said five others disappeared. This guy makes one, so there might be four others. I'm not sure what to suggest to you."

"We will do what we should have done with your friend," said Ruth. "We will invite them in and try to explain to them what happened."

"We'll teach them the ways of the new world they've encountered," said Bill. "You've heard of the underground railroad? This will be the underground railroad for time travelers." He shook his head. "I just wish we had done right by Pete."

"It's okay," said Alice. "It was just as scary for you as it was for him. I don't think any of us hold it against you."

But Keith had no doubt that Bill and Ruth would be haunted by their actions for the rest of their lives.

Chapter 27

By late May, they were ready to leave. It was still cold at night, but most of the snow had melted from a stretch of sunny, warm days. While their stay at the Inn had been comfortable, they were more than ready to move on. Besides, Ruth and Bill had to prepare for their first guests of the year the following week.

The flu pandemic hadn't hit the rural areas yet and hadn't made the newspapers in February and March, but Keith, Alice, and Nicholas knew that they had to be careful in their travels. Keith read in the newspaper in April that a number of soldiers in Kansas had come down with the flu a few weeks earlier.

"I think I remember reading that the outbreak at the military base in Kansas was thought to have been the start of the pandemic," said Nicholas. "One theory, anyway. If we leave soon, we might make it to Nebraska before things get bad."

The question, of course, was how to get there. They still had no money and felt badly that they had sponged off Ruth and Bill for so long.

"If we can get to Boston, I'll get us some money," said Nicholas. "When we get to Nebraska, we can send them whatever we have left over before we enter the portal."

Keith didn't want to ask Nicholas how he would get the money but knew that whatever it was wouldn't be legal. But Ray had mentioned in his note that sometimes they would just have to do what was necessary.

However, the first step was to get to Boston.

"I think I can help you there," said Bill when they mentioned their dilemma to him. "We have a delivery coming tomorrow. We're last on his schedule, then he heads back to Boston. I'll ask if you can ride back with him in the truck. It's a nice truck—a new model. It's a brand new 1918 Chevrolet."

"Thank you," said Keith. "And thank you both for your hospitality. I know we put you out and ate a lot of your food. When we get to where we're going, we'll get some money together and send it to you."

"If you can, we'd certainly appreciate it," said Ruth. "But if not, at least you've given us an experience of a lifetime—not that we can tell anyone, of course."

"They'd probably lock you up," said Keith with a laugh.

When the delivery arrived the next day, Bill introduced them to Rory, a stocky man in his forties whose hat hung over one eye. Rory agreed to take them but warned them that the back of the truck—a flatbed—would be cold and uncomfortable. He invited Alice to sit in the cab, which would be warmer. She thanked him for his kindness but said she was happy back with her husband.

Sensing the morality of the time, Keith and Alice chose to pose as husband and wife. In fact, they were getting closer by the week. When they first met, Keith saw Alice as a typical college airhead. But in the many weeks since their "discussion," he had begun to realize her depth. He mentioned it to her the night before their journey to Boston. They were lying on Keith's bed in the dark. It was now almost six months since they had gone through the portal. They would often lie in bed together and talk. It brought them both a lot of comfort.

"I think everyone in college is an airhead to some degree," said Alice. "Maybe it's one of the requirements of college. I think it's because most students still haven't figured out what they want to do with their life. The ones who have a clear goal are the serious ones. The rest of us are hoping inspiration strikes us at some point. I'm in graduate school—or, I was—majoring in Social Work, but I was still waiting for the inspiration."

"Do you think about Barbara much?" asked Keith.

"Sometimes, but not as much as I thought I would. She knew what she wanted, and she went for it. I do wonder where she is, and I miss our girl talk sessions. But I found you, and that's more important. Do you think about Cyndi a lot?"

Keith was quiet for a minute before answering. Alice began to wonder if he'd fallen asleep. Or worse, that she shouldn't have asked the question. When he finally spoke, it was almost a whisper.

"I do, but not in the way you might think. Of course, I wonder how she's doing, and I miss things we did together. But sometimes I wonder what I would do if we ever did make it home. I love Cyndi and always will, but I'm also falling in love with you. I know this sounds cowardly, but maybe it's good that our chances of making it home are slim—maybe it's not a decision I will ever have to make."

That night, they made love for the first time.

*****

Rory wasn't kidding. The back of the truck was uncomfortable, but they didn't complain. He was getting them to Boston—granted, at a snail's pace—and they all appreciated it.

"Do I dare ask how you are going to get us money?" Keith asked Nicholas.

"You can ask," answered Nicholas. "This might give you a hint." He pulled a semi-automatic pistol from behind his back.

"Whoa," said Keith, "where did you get that?"

"I've always had it," answered Nicholas. "I just never showed it to you."

"You had it when we were exploring the building?"

"I did."

"Do you carry it for a reason or just because you can?"

"A reason."

"One that you'd like to share?"

"No."

"Nicholas, we've been together for six months, and I know nothing more about you than I did the first day we met. Can you open up a bit?"

"Let's just say I had some dangerous people coming after me. Unless they send their ancestors, that's the last I'll ever see of them. But I procured the gun, just in case."

"Ancestors? Care to elaborate?" Keith asked.

"I will, but not now."

*****

They reached Boston that evening, stiff and exhausted. Bill had pulled Rory aside before they left and told him his passengers couldn't pay him, so there wasn't much awkwardness. Bill had also lied, using the story about Keith having had polio as a child to explain why he wasn't in the military. That was the story Keith would use if questioned by anyone.

Bill had given them enough money for one night in a cheap hotel. He didn't ask how they would get money for train tickets west but knew that Nicholas would somehow get it. Keith had noticed that Bill and Ruth were always a little scared of Nicholas, even though he wasn't an imposing figure. Something about him caused people to give him a wide berth.

Bill had been wrong about how much money they'd need. They found two rooms in a decent hotel with money left to buy a nice dinner.

"Keep the hotel for another couple of nights," Nicholas said after dinner. "We'll have to lay low to let things calm down. I have to go take care of something right now."

"Are you going to rob a bank?" asked Alice.

"At 8:00 at night? No. Besides, we don't need that much money. And robbing a bank is a big deal with the police. I'll find the right bar and hit it as they're closing. Less interest on the part of the police. Less risk for me."

"There's no other way?" asked Alice.

"No."

"Want help?" asked Keith, hoping Nicholas would say no. Nicholas didn't disappoint.

"Thanks, but it's a job done better alone. Besides, if something goes wrong—which it won't—you and Alice have a life to get on with. Anyway, gotta go."

When they left the restaurant, Nicholas had stolen a coat, hat, and scarf. He carried them with him now as he left the room. Keith assumed they would be used as a disguise.

"Don't wait up for me," said Nicholas.

Chapter 28

The night had turned chilly, so Nicholas put on the coat, hat, and scarf. The coat was two sizes too large, but it gave him room to hide the gun. Besides, it made him look heavyset. The police wouldn't be looking for a man as thin as Nicholas. He'd ditch the outfit when he was safely away from the bar.

He began his search around 9:00 p.m., concentrating on the working-class section of Boston. His goal was simple—look for a bar that was busy but not too busy, and one that catered to a better clientele of the working class. A dingy bar that attracted drunks and drifters wouldn't have much cash on hand. An upscale bar would have the cash but would also become the focus of too much attention if he robbed it. An anonymous tavern doing a steady business was his goal. Luckily, prohibition was still two years away, so bars were plentiful.

Just before midnight, he found it. The bar was on a quiet street with a steady stream of customers. He watched from a secluded spot across the street, noting the number of workers and their physical characteristics—too many burly guys would make it difficult.

This bar had three older men tending bar and cleaning and a middle-aged woman waiting tables. By 2:00 a.m., the crowd had thinned to a couple of customers slumped over the bar in an alcoholic blackout. The waitress had gone home an hour earlier.

It was time.

Nicholas pulled out his .45 from behind his back. He took a silencer from his pocket and screwed it onto the gun. The less noise, the better—but hopefully, he wouldn't have to use it. Then, he wrapped the scarf around the lower part of his face.

As he entered the bar, one of the bartenders called out that they were closing.

"I'll just be a minute," said Nicholas, raising his gun.

"Whoa, hey, buddy, none of that."

"I don't need all your money," said Nicholas. "A hundred should be enough."

"A hundred? That's more than we took in all night."

The three men behind the bar didn't look scared. That wasn't good.

"What the hell is on your gun?" asked one of them.

"It's a silencer—a suppressor—I could shoot all three of you, and no one would hear it."

"Bullshit," said the oldest of the bunch, chewing a chaw of tobacco.

Nicholas aimed at a lamp across the room and pulled the trigger. There was a muffled crack from the gun, and the lamp exploded.

"Holy shit!" said the man, almost choking on his tobacco.

But while Nicholas was aiming at the lamp, one of the other men lifted a shotgun from under the counter. Nicholas turned just as the man pointed it toward him.

Quickly, Nicholas took a shot, and a red hole appeared in the man's forehead. The man slumped to the floor.

"Sam!" cried out the tobacco-chewer. "You killed Sam."

"Wasn't my intention," said Nicholas. "It's only money. He didn't have to do that. But since he did, give me everything you have and make it quick. Put it in a bag."

The men did as he asked, and a minute later, Nicholas was out the door.

He walked quickly to the corner. No one was on the street, so he shed his coat, hat, and scarf, and stuffed them in a trash bin. He took the money from the bag, folded the bills, and put them in his right pocket. He divided the change between his other three pockets and threw away the bag. He took off the silencer, put it in the pocket with the bills, and put the gun in his pants behind his back. He untucked the shirt to cover the gun.

When Nicholas reached the hotel, he immediately went to his room, where he counted the money—$175. The guy lied about $100 being more than they took in, but not by much.

Was he bothered by the killing? A little, but the man brought it on himself. He didn't need to do that. Besides, Nicholas had killed many people—one more wouldn't matter. But this one was different. Would it affect the future in any way? Ray had written in his note that the jury was out on that. Well, it didn't matter now.

What was done was done.

Chapter 29

Keith and Alice had spent the night making love. Once the ice had been broken on their last day in New Hampshire, there was no holding back. For Alice, it was love, but it was also the comfort and safety she had been seeking. For Keith, it was also those things, but tempered with an overriding deep sense of guilt.

Stepping out on Cyndi was something he never would have done. But what were the chances he'd ever see her again? One percent? Zero percent? And how long should he wait before moving on with his life? Should he wait until they had gone through another portal? Two portals? Ray said the chances of ever making it home were slim, but Keith was sure that Ray was saying that to let them hold onto a bit of hope. Ray knew that they'd never make it home—he just couldn't put it into words and dash their hopes completely.

The fact was, Keith wasn't cheating on Cyndi. He wasn't on vacation or a business trip cheating with a coworker—he was restarting his whole life. He had to remember the good times with Cyndi and move on. All he could hope for was that Cyndi would eventually restart her life. He had hinted at that in his note to her. He knew that she had been in contact with Ray. Hopefully, Ray was honest with her and didn't leave her with any false hope. Based on Ray's note, Keith thought he'd tell Cyndi the truth. That was good.

Keith looked down at Alice, now sound asleep. The moonlight shining through the window illuminated her face. Her expression was one of contentment. Keith was her rock in the chaos that was time travel. Keith was happy that he could be that for her.

Something she hadn't realized yet but would soon enough was that she was Keith's rock. Without her, his life would be barren. He would be stuck somewhere in time without a lifeline.

Alice was that lifeline.

*****

Nicholas knocked softly on their door at 9:00 the next morning. They were up and ready for him. Keith opened the door and ushered him in. Nicholas set the pile of bills on the bed.

"I also have a lot of change that we can split later. It'll be better if we split all the money among us. There's about $175. That'll easily get us to Nebraska, and we can send some to Ruth and Bill. We can also take some of it with us through the portal. After all, it'll still be good in 1950."

"Did it go well?" asked Keith.

"Well enough."

"What does that mean?"

"It means we got the money, and they're looking for a guy in a big coat, a hat, and a scarf covering his face. We're in the clear, but I want to give it another day or so before we leave."

"We're going out for breakfast," said Keith, "Want to join us?"

"No, I'm going back to bed. Also, it's probably better to let things calm down for the day. Maybe later, I'll have you bring me back something."

"I'll be happy to."

Keith was glad that he had the time alone with Alice. Besides, there was something he wanted to do, and he didn't want Nicholas with him when he did it.

By the time they left the hotel, it was mid-morning, so they decided to walk around the city, comparing it to the Boston they had known. It was a sunny day, and they felt good. Despite the shock of living a hundred years in the past, giving up all they'd known, they felt surprisingly free. The love they felt for each other was real. Keith even wondered if his love for Alice was stronger than his love for Cyndi. He felt guilty even thinking it, but it was a real feeling that he couldn't ignore. It also wasn't fair to Cyndi. What he had with Alice was a new love, which was always exciting. His love for Cyndi was established—they'd had a few years to hone it.

They ate lunch at an outdoor restaurant, then roamed the city some more. The city was different from the Boston they knew, but at the same time, it was familiar. Landmarks that they considered old in 2026 were shiny and new. The Boston Common was surprisingly similar to the Common that they knew. They rode the subway and the elevated train, laughingly comparing it to the "T" system that they were used to. Late in the afternoon, Keith stopped at a newsstand. The afternoon edition of the *Boston Globe* had to be out by now. It was, so Keith bought it, and then they went to a park to sit and read it.

Keith was looking for something and found it on the front page. The headline read: *One man dead in brazen bar robbery.*

Just as he suspected, Nicholas had killed a man!

Alice read it, too.

"What are we going to do?" she asked.

"Nothing. I think it best if we don't bring it up. We've felt for a long time that Nicholas was dangerous. This confirms it. At some point, we'll split from him. Until then, I think it's best not to let on that we know. Besides, we don't know the situation. Maybe he had no choice. We'll let him bring it up if he wants. In the meantime, let's prepare to go to Nebraska."

They headed back to the hotel and were passing an alley when two men jumped out, grabbed them, and pushed them into the shadows. Keith and Alice both landed on their backs.

The two men approached menacingly, one of them brandishing an old pistol. They were young—probably no older than Alice—and wore caps down low, almost covering their eyes.

"Give us your money, and we won't kill you."

Keith and Alice slowly got to their feet.

Keith had seen their type before. Their goal was to scare their victims and hope for a quick score.

Keith looked at Alice, expecting her to be trembling. Instead, she was staring at the man in front of her without fear.

Speaking to the hood in front of him—the one with the gun—Keith said, "You won't kill us."

"Why?"

"Because the barrel of your gun is clogged with dirt."

The man lifted his gun to look at the barrel, and Keith kicked out, knocking the gun from the man's hand. Then he spun and landed a roundhouse kick to the man's head, dropping him to the ground.

Alice, meanwhile, jumped at the man in front of her, whose attention was momentarily taken by the attack on his friend. Alice kneed him in the groin. As he bent over in pain, she grabbed his head, brought her knee up, and smashed his nose. He dropped to the ground, squealing and holding his nose with one hand and his groin with the other.

Keith kicked his attacker's gun into a corner, then stared at Alice.

"Bet you thought I was just a helpless female," she said.

He shook his head slowly in amazement.

"Not anymore."

They decided to leave the men to nurse their injuries. Both were still writhing in pain.

"We should go back to the hotel," said Alice, amused that Keith was still somewhat speechless. Keith nodded and followed her out to the sidewalk.

Two days later, they were on a train headed west.

*****

Nicholas never brought up the incident at the bar. In fact, he remained strangely silent for most of the long trip west. Was he feeling guilty about killing the man? Keith couldn't be sure, but somehow, Nicholas didn't seem the type to have feelings of guilt or regret. Maybe he was feeling the same nervousness that Keith and Alice had about going through another portal.

The portal was something Keith and Alice had talked about several times. The fear was real. Ray had said that they needed to be touching to land together. But what if it didn't work? What if they arrived months apart? They devised a temporary plan to visit the train station at the same time every day if that were to happen. When Keith mentioned it to Nicholas, he nodded his head in agreement.

"Look, I don't know about you two," said Nicholas, "but I'd rather not stay in this time any longer than necessary. I'd rather move on to a time that feels a little more familiar. Where's the next portal?"

"Outside the town of Fremont," said Keith. "The train goes right through Fremont. You probably didn't even look at your ticket. I agree with you. The sooner we go through, the better."

When they finally reached Fremont, they were exhausted. It was early evening, so they decided to stay the night in a hotel and leave the next morning. They would also stop by the post office and mail $50 in cash to Ruth and Bill, leaving them a little bit to use when they hit 1950.

But things didn't go exactly as planned.

Chapter 30

When they got off the train, they asked the ticket agent where to find a hotel for the night. They were directed to a hotel in the center of town.

As they left the station, Keith whispered to Nicholas that someone was watching them.

"He's in the corner," said Keith. "He's holding a newspaper, but it just makes him stand out."

Alice heard what he said and added quietly, "I saw him, too, and was going to tell you. He looks like someone from a cheap spy movie."

"Could he be one of the people who were chasing you?" Keith asked Nicholas.

"Impossible. I don't see how. But I'll keep an eye on him. You're both right. He looks suspicious. Maybe he's just a crook looking for his next mark."

They never made it to the hotel.

They had just dropped the letter to Ruth and Bill in the mailbox in front of the post office when Alice cried out. Something went through the sleeve of her jacket and put a hole in the mailbox.

"What was that?" cried Keith. "Are you okay, Alice?"

"I'm fine. It went through my jacket. It didn't hit me."

"No time for that," said Nicholas. "Move, move, move!"

He pushed them out of the way just as another hole appeared in the mailbox. This time, they all heard a popping noise before the hole appeared.

They took cover behind a parked car, and Nicholas pulled out his gun. Three holes appeared in succession in the front seat of the car.

"No time for the silencer," said Nicholas, who took aim at a target across the street and took two shots. The noise from the .45 put an end to the quiet of the evening. Pedestrians screamed and took cover.

Two more pops sounded from across the street, and one of the tires of the car they hid behind exploded.

"We have to get out of here," said Keith. "I see some cops coming."

Nicholas aimed and shot three times. The first shot destroyed the shooter's weapon and his hand. The second shot got the man in the throat. As he was falling, Nicholas's third shot put a hole in his forehead.

"Let's go," shouted Keith.

Nicholas hesitated. It looked to Keith like he was considering going across the street to check out the shooter.

"Nicholas, he's dead. Let's go."

Still, Nicholas hesitated. Finally, with the police less than a block away, he shook his head and said quietly, "Okay, you're right. Let's go."

They ran up the street in the general direction of the portal. People stepped out of their way. One man foolishly tried to stop them, but Nicholas smashed him in the face with his gun. The man screamed in pain.

"Stupid," muttered Nicholas.

"What were you doing back there?" asked Keith as they ran. "It looked like you wanted to go over to the shooter."

"I did. I wanted a better look at him."

"I thought you said no one else was coming after you."

"Obviously, I was wrong."

Keith let it go. Nicholas was angry. The more questions Keith asked, the angrier Nicholas was going to become.

What Keith wanted to ask Nicholas was about the shooter's weapon. Was he using a silencer? Keith had never heard that kind of pop before, except maybe with a Nerf gun. But that was no Nerf gun.

They were on the outskirts of town now. A hundred yards away, on their left, was an abandoned barn. Keith pointed to it. Nicholas nodded, and they all headed for it.

They were tired and needed to rest. They had left the pedestrians behind them, and hopefully the police, as well. Keith figured the police would spend a few minutes with the dead man before continuing their pursuit.

"We can't stay here long," said Nicholas. "We don't want to get surrounded, and I don't want to kill a cop."

"Speaking of which," said Keith, "that was some pretty amazing shooting, getting the guy in the throat and forehead, and destroying his weapon."

"Yes," answered Nicholas.

That was all Keith was going to get from him.

Keith pulled out the Portal Finder and turned it on. He looked at the screen and announced, "We're almost there. We're close."

"Then we should go," said Alice.

They picked up their backpacks and headed back to the road.

"It's less than a mile."

"It better be a quick mile," said Nicholas. "They see us."

Shouts from their pursuers were punctuated by the occasional pistol being fired. Keith wasn't sure if they were shooting in the air or aiming for them, and he didn't want to stop to find out.

By the time they had gone the mile, they were exhausted.

"It's off to the side," said Keith.

They suddenly came upon a chasm in the earth between two large rocks.

"It's down at the bottom, in the corner," said Keith.

They helped each other down the steep slope until they were standing at the bottom. They heard the huffing and puffing of the police behind them.

"We have to go now," said Nicholas, inching toward the corner. "Don't forget to hold hands."

"I'm scared," said Alice.

"We're all scared," replied Nicholas. "But we have no choice."

"It's right here," said Keith. "Let's go."

They took five steps.

Suddenly, there was music, talking, and laughing. They had made it through! All around them were empty liquor bottles and beer cans. Something was going on at the top of the crevasse. It sounded like a party. Well, they had no choice—they couldn't stay where they were. They carefully climbed the steep slope.

When they reached the top, everything went dead silent.

Keith looked around and saw about two dozen young people. They all had drinks in their hands, and most were smoking.

And they were all staring at them.

"Excuse us," said Keith. "We're just passing through."

He led the way through the stunned teens to a hole in a fence that hadn't been there in 1917.

Alice laughed. "They had no idea what just happened."

"Did we make it to 1950?" asked Nicholas.

Keith looked at the Portal Finder. "We did. April 3rd, 1950."

They started walking toward town. It seemed to be about midday.

"Where do we go now?" asked Nicholas.

"I don't know," answered Keith. "We can look when we get to town. It would probably be best to put as much distance between the kids and us as possible. One of them will eventually come to his senses and might want to do something, like contact the authorities."

Keith looked down at his 1917 clothes.

"We do look a little out of place."

"Ray said we should change into appropriate clothes before going through a portal, but the police didn't give us enough time," said Alice.

"With that in mind," began Keith. "Have you figured—"

"No," answered Nicholas. "When I do, I'll let you know."

Keith suddenly realized just how bothered by the shooter Nicholas was. There was something about it that confused Nicholas. He was adamant that no one else would be coming after him. *Not unless it was their ancestor,* he said. Tonight, Nicholas was going to have to open up with them. After all, their lives were now in jeopardy, too.

"We need clothes and then a place to stay," said Alice, pointing to a clothing store down the block from a hotel.

"Hey," said Keith with a laugh, moving on from his conversation with Nicholas, "that's the hotel we were going to stay in 33 years ago. I wonder if they still have our reservation. So, clothes and then a place to stay."

"Then," said Alice, "you can look at your magic machine from the future to see where we go next."

Chapter 31

AT SEA—JANUARY 1918

Private Pete Green sat on his bunk with a bucket beside him in the belly of the troop transport ship *Agamemnon*. The ship was pitching and rolling in the churning seas. Pete had lost his breakfast and the previous night's dinner and still felt sick. It was worse when he laid down, and it was too violent to get up and walk. So, he sat there, sad, lonely, and sick.

The ship, a captured German passenger steamship formerly called *Kaiser Wilhelm II* and renamed the *Agamemnon* by the Secretary of the Navy, had left Hoboken on its second voyage to France five days earlier, and the sailing had been relatively calm—until today. There had been talk of a man overboard earlier in the day, but that was just an unfounded rumor. Pete didn't care. He cared about very little these days.

After the old reservist had taken him to Manchester to sign up, he was immediately driven to Camp Devens in Massachusetts for some brief training. Devens wasn't far from where he grew up, but of course, Massachusetts looked nothing like he knew it. It was mostly farms and dirt roads.

On the ride down to Manchester, Pete had tried to explain to the old guy and the sheriff's deputy that he was from another time, but it fell on deaf ears (literally, in the old reservist's case). The deputy told him that if he brought it up again, he would be beaten within an inch of his life.

Pete threw up into his bucket again. When he brought his head up, he saw a man standing in an open hatch staring at him.

Him again, thought Pete. He had caught the man looking at him several times over the past few days. He was part of a different regiment, maybe even a different division. He wasn't sure. All he knew was that the man was berthed in another section of the ship. But somehow, he made it a point to watch Pete. It was getting creepy. Was the guy attracted to him?

The guy had disappeared. Pete would make sure to confront him the next time. For now, he just felt too sick.

Two days later, the *Agamemnon* docked in France. Pete was happy to finally get off the ship and feel real ground under him again.

Several regiments had set up camp in the same area while awaiting orders. Pete was leaving a latrine when he saw the man staring at him from some nearby trees. Most of the soldiers were young—even younger than Pete—but this man was older. However, he wasn't an officer. He was an enlisted man like Pete.

Enough! He had to find out why the man was so interested in him. As he began walking toward the trees, the man slipped from view. Now Pete ran. As he reached the trees, he saw the man heading in the opposite direction toward one of the other regiments. The man was only about twenty yards ahead of him.

"Hey," yelled Pete, "wait up."

The man stopped and slowly turned, and Pete finally got a good look at him. He had to be in his forties, far beyond the age of most enlisted men. His hair had gone prematurely gray, and the lines etched on his face were those of someone who had experienced a lot—and much of it not good.

"Why do you keep looking at me?" asked Pete.

"What do you mean?"

The man tried to give off an innocent aura, but he was anything but innocent.

"You know what I mean. Every time I turn around, I see you looking at me. Do I look like someone you know?"

"No, I'm sorry that I've been watching you, but I had to convince myself of something, and I think I have. When are you from?"

"What?"

"When are you from?"

Pete didn't know how to answer the question. The last time he tried to tell someone he was from the future, he ended up in France, preparing to fight the Germans. It would be best to get the other man talking.

"Why do you ask that question?"

"Because you're not supposed to be here."

"Well, duh, none of us are."

"They didn't use the expression, 'duh' in 1918. I would guess you're from at least the 1970s."

"Who are you?" asked Pete.

"I'm one of you," came the answer.

"One of me, what?"

"A time traveler."

Pete knew it was coming, but he flinched anyway. Remaining silent seemed like the best option, so he chose it.

"You don't know if you can trust me. I get it. I understand. But who in 1918 would accuse you of being a time traveler?"

"Let's go about this a different way," said Pete. "Who are you?"

"My name is Charlie—at least, that's the name I use. I'm from the year 2116. I came back in time as an Eliminator."

"A what?"

"Just as I thought," said Charlie, "you're not a professional time traveler."

"They have *professional* time travelers?"

"Let me correct that to *intentional* time traveler. Do you know Hanna or Simone?"

"Never heard of them."

"They were from my time, part of the Time Travel Project. The last I knew, Hanna and Simone hooked up with some accidental time travelers, Alex Frost, Ray Burton..."

"*That* name I know. He had just returned to 2025 from time traveling. He became quite famous—he and Natalie O'Brien, the actress, and some other guy."

"So, they made it home," said Charlie. "Good for them. That's rare—almost unheard of."

"So, I'll ask again," said Pete, "what's an Eliminator? It sounds ominous, like an assassin."

"That's exactly what it is," said Charlie. "My job was to come back in time and eliminate time travelers. It was decided that having people stuck in time was dangerous to the future. So, if I were still an Eliminator, my job right now would be to say, 'You're not supposed to be here,' and then eliminate you."

"In other words, kill me."

"Right."

"But you referred to it in the past tense. I take it you're not an Eliminator any longer?"

"That would be correct."

"Why?"

"Simply stated, I didn't have the stomach for it. I found my first subject, held my weapon to her head, and couldn't pull the trigger. All my training went out the window."

When Pete didn't say anything, Charlie continued.

"That was in the year 1948. It was my second stop in my time travel journey."

"What was your first stop?"

"It was 2010. I was supposed to take care of some of the original time travelers from the Time Travel Project: Max Hawkins, Alan Garland, and Herb Wells. Any of those names seem familiar?"

"No."

"Doesn't matter. I was just curious how much you knew."

"Pretty much nothing."

"I can see that."

It was an insult, but Pete didn't think it was intentional, so he left it alone.

"Anyway, Hawkins and Wells had already moved on—meaning they went through a portal—and I couldn't find Garland. I found a portal here in France that took me to 1948 and another traveler. That's where I botched my mission. I found another portal to take me to 1967, but I ended up in 1917 instead. I don't understand how that could've happened."

"How…?"

"How did I find the portals? Something called a Portal Finder. You don't need to know the specifics. Anyway, I took the mistake as a sign. I'd always been fascinated with the First World War, so I decided to stay. I don't have much longer to live, and figured I'd see what the war was all about."

"Why won't you live?"

"Long story that I won't bore you with, but I have a disease known as MMD—Male Midlife Disease. I won't live past fifty and could keel over any time between now and then. Since I'm a dead man anyway, I thought, 'Why not?' So, I destroyed my Portal Finder and weapon and joined the war. They didn't seem to care that I was older. I guess they are desperate."

"Why did you destroy the Portal Finder and weapon?"

"Didn't want them found. Can't leave any trace of the future. And the weapon could be dangerous in the wrong hands."

"How did you know I was not from this time?" asked Pete.

"Something about your mannerisms got me curious. They seemed wrong, somehow incongruent with the early 1900s. Then, as I looked at you more closely, it was your ears."

"My ears?"

"We read in our history books that men in the late 20th and early 21st centuries had a strange attraction to the round things in your ears—gauges, that's what they were called. The only others who did that to their ears were some African tribes and early Egyptian, Mayan, and Aztec civilizations. You didn't belong to any of those, so you must've been from the 21st century."

"But I don't have gauges."

"You must have had them at some point because you have the remnants of holes in your earlobes, holes not caused by regular earrings. I noticed them when I was behind you in a chow line."

"I experimented with gauges in my late teens, but it didn't last long."

"Long enough to leave holes that are still closing. They'd probably be missed by most people, but we were trained to be observant and gather all clues. Anyway, it was enough to make you stand out in my mind."

*****

The two regiments remained side by side for the next two weeks, awaiting orders to move. During that time, Pete and Charlie spent all their free time together. Charlie told Pete about all of the significant events of the middle and latter half of the 21st century, and Pete told Charlie what it was like living in the early part of the century.

Pete was happy to have found someone he could talk to. It relieved a little of the loneliness, but only a little. Charlie admitted that he, too, was lonely for intelligent conversation. He felt that while there were men all around him that were smart, they were smart for their time, and would never be able to relate to the experiences that he'd had. While Pete didn't have the knowledge that Charlie had, just being a child of the 21st century brought him that much closer to Charlie's time.

For Pete, it was two weeks of respite from the hell he'd experienced since arriving in 1917.

And then the orders came.

Pete and Charlie were going into battle.

Chapter 32

Pete and Charlie said goodbye to each other the day they headed off to the real war—the war where men actually die. Even though the regiments would be fighting next to each other, there were thousands of soldiers involved. They knew they might never see each other again.

Once his unit reached its assigned location—a mile-wide empty field that had once been a farm—they were told to dig foxholes. Pete shared a foxhole with two other men. The three had seen each other around but had never had a conversation. Both of the others were named Jack, but one was from Texas, so Pete and the other Jack called him Tex. Tex was seventeen—a very scared seventeen—and Jack was closer to Pete's age but no less scared.

"Where are you from?" Jack asked Pete.

"Boston."

"Oh yeah? I'm from Nashua."

"I was actually in North Conway when I signed up," said Pete.

"That's funny," said Jack. "Did you have an old deaf guy sign you up?"

"I did. Can't remember his name, though."

"Me neither, but he was telling a story about a guy he signed up from North Conway who kept insisting that he was from the future."

"I heard that story, too," said Pete. "I guess you get all kinds."

"Yeah," said Tex. "Just this morning, I heard that a guy in the other regiment died suddenly. Wasn't shot or nothin'. He just died. An older guy. They said he musta died from fear. Heart attack or sumthin."

Pete didn't need to be told who it was. Charlie's disease had caught up with him. Well, maybe it was better that way. He wasn't shot or blown up. It was a peaceful death. Pete kind of envied him.

They spent the first night huddled in the foxhole. The night was clear, and the enemy hadn't arrived.

"Quiet," said Tex.

"Almost too quiet," added Jack.

Pete chuckled.

"What?" asked Jack.

"Oh, nothing. That's what they always say in the mov…in the books. You know, like Westerns when they're waiting for the Indians to attack."

"I read a Western last year by some guy named Zane Grey. Ever hearda him?" asked Tex.

"Yeah," said Jack, chastising himself for almost saying the wrong thing again. He was beginning to realize just how hard it was to travel through time without giving himself away.

An hour later, his two foxhole mates were sound asleep. Pete couldn't sleep, however. He was thinking about Barbara and Alice—but mostly Barbara. He was missing her terribly. He thought about the last time they made love, the night before the exploration. He'd never touch her body again. It made him sad. He would never see her or anyone from his old life again.

At the same time, he realized that he had finally accepted his situation. He was never going home. This was his life now, and it sucked. Maybe dying here wouldn't be so bad. After all, he had nothing to look forward to. With that thought, he realized that he wasn't scared anymore. If he died in battle, he died in battle. It gave him a new perspective.

He finally fell asleep in the middle of the night.

By morning, it had clouded over. They went to the mess tent to pick up breakfast and bring it back to the foxhole. On their way back, it began to rain. Within minutes, it was pouring. By the time they reached the foxhole, their breakfast was soggy, and the hole had six inches of water in the bottom. It was going to be an uncomfortable day.

The rain came in buckets. By noon, despite their attempts to bail water from the foxhole—using their helmets—they were up to their waists in cold, muddy water.

Then Pete heard a "fwump" in the distance. A few seconds later, there was an explosion less than fifty feet from their foxhole. Mud rained down on them. Pete and the others covered their heads and quickly put their helmets back on.

Then there was another explosion. And another. The battle had begun.

For three hours, mortar shells exploded all around them. A foxhole only thirty feet away from them caught a direct hit, and a man's arm landed next to Pete. All three men threw up at the sight of it. Pete picked it up and tossed it away from the foxhole.

Not a shot was fired during the three-hour attack—there was no one to shoot at. The cannons and mortars were on the other side of the tree line. Their own cannons and mortars were firing back, but Pete had no idea if they were doing any damage to the enemy.

Suddenly, the explosions stopped. A few men cheered, but most didn't. They knew better. It was only going to get worse from there.

For several hours, calm prevailed. Then, from the woods came gunshots—hundreds of them all at once. Pete heard the screams of the men who were hit. A sergeant was yelling something, but Pete couldn't catch the words. Men from the other foxholes began to fire, so he, Jack, and Tex joined in. The enemy was too far away to aim at specific targets, so Pete just shot into the approaching crowd and hoped for the best.

The onslaught continued for at least an hour. None of the Germans made it as far as Pete's foxhole, but it didn't mean that the bullets weren't flying around them. Pete kept his head down and only raised it to take a shot.

Finally, the enemy retreated, and Pete laid back against the side of the foxhole. But it was only for a moment. The rain hadn't let up, and Pete and the others had to get back to the process of bailing.

Pete was frozen, especially from the waist down. It was still winter, and even though it was raining and not snowing, he was chilled to the bone.

A corporal appeared at the edge of the foxhole.

"The captain wants you to abandon this hole and move up closer to the front—and do it quick."

They gathered their belongings and climbed out of the hole. Pete didn't want to move closer to the action, but he had no choice. They found an empty foxhole fifty yards closer to the woods. It was just as wet as their other one had been.

The afternoon dragged on. At dinner time, they were told to take turns going for chow, eat it quickly, and return to the foxhole. Pete and Tex let Jack go first.

"Don't eat all the steak," said Tex. "Save some for us."

"Steak? Ha! Don't make me laugh."

Jack had only gone twenty feet when a shot rang out from the woods.

"Ooof." Jack fell to his knees. Another shot, and he fell to the ground.

"Jack!" yelled Pete, just as the cannons and mortars started up again.

"You stay here," he said to Tex.

Shots rang out again from the woods. He ran to his friend. Jack was still breathing.

"Hang in there, buddy," said Pete. "You'll be fine."

Suddenly, there was an explosion right next to them. Pete was hurled several feet. He cried out as he landed. There were pains in every part of his body. He looked back at Jack. The man was dead, a piece of shrapnel sticking out from the side of his head.

Pete was in pain. He slid over to a foxhole with two dead soldiers in it and fell in beside them. He heard screaming and looked up to see his comrades retreating. He caught a glimpse of Tex, who had left his rifle behind and was running for his life. Pete quickly lay down in the water and mud and pulled the two dead men over him. And then he passed out.

Chapter 33

Pete remembered hands on him and then being dragged out of the foxhole. He remembered being put on a stretcher and carried off the battlefield. There was no more shooting. Who won the battle? Did Tex survive? Again, he passed out.

The pain was unbearable, and Pete went in and out of consciousness. During one of his semi-lucid moments, he heard, "Take the leg." Where were they going to take it? Another time, he was lying in his bed at home, and his mother was telling him that it would be okay. He hadn't lived at home since high school. What was his mother doing there?

It was cold—so cold! And his arms wouldn't move. Then he realized that he was strapped down. Why? Needles—he saw men with big needles, and they were hovering over his leg. It was the leg that hurt so much.

He passed out again.

He woke to a man standing over him. And there was a strange noise—like sawing wood. And then he felt it—a pain unlike any he'd ever felt. Pete screamed. He heard the man call out, "What's this man doing awake?"

There was blood all over the place.

Pete screamed again … and again. And then there was nothing.

*****

Pete opened his eyes. Well, one eye. There was a bandage covering the other. Everything hurt. He had a pounding headache, and pains in his side and chest. He was having a little trouble breathing. Mostly, though, the pain in his left leg was unbearable.

He was moving. He looked around and saw two men lying on cots attached to the wall. He was in an ambulance. The vehicle hit a pothole, and he cried out. The other two men didn't—they were unconscious. Another pothole and another cry. The road was terrible. He heard the tires sloshing through the mud.

"Oh, you're awake. How do you feel?"

It was a woman's voice. She sounded young and kind.

"Everything hurts," he whispered.

"Are you thirsty?"

He nodded.

She put a glass to his lips. Some of the water splashed down his neck, but he got enough to satisfy his thirst.

"Where am I?"

"You're going to a hospital—well, what passes for a hospital. More like a field hospital. Your wounds were very bad, and they had to do surgery in the medical tent. Considering the conditions, they did a good job."

"My leg is killing me."

"Really? They didn't list that as one of your wounds."

She felt his right leg.

"No, the other leg."

The nurse looked at him with a sad expression.

"I'm sorry," she looked at his chart, "Pete. They had to take that leg. If they hadn't, you would have died."

Flashbacks of the operation suddenly came to mind. He remembered someone saying something about taking the leg.

They were talking about *his* leg?

"Nooo, that can't be. I feel it. It's there."

"I'm sorry."

He must have passed out again, because the next thing he knew, he was in a different bed in a large room. The bed was slightly more comfortable than the cot in the ambulance, but not by much. He no longer had the bandage on his head.

He felt dizzy and weak—so weak.

A young doctor stopped to examine his wounds. Seeing that Pete was awake, he gave him a tired smile.

"Pete Green. Is that your name?"

"Yes." His voice was hoarse.

"Well, Pete, you lost a lot of blood. We were able to give you a little blood using a new process called blood transfusion. But it wasn't much. It's kind of new around here. Considering the circumstances, the doctors at the front line did a decent job of amputating your leg. But I'll be honest with you. The leg isn't what worries me. Your side and chest suffered a lot of shrapnel damage. Some of the shrapnel is still in there, in places too dangerous to operate. We're worried about blood poisoning, so we have to keep watching it."

"And if I get blood poisoning?" Pete whispered. But he already knew the answer to that.

"There's no easy way to say this, but you could die. But let's hope for the best."

A cry came from a bed down the line, and the doctor excused himself.

The best. What was the best he could look forward to? Sitting on the sidewalk with a can, looking for handouts? What would he do? As it was, even if he were healthy, he would have a hard time finding work. He didn't know anything about this time period. Maybe they had taught it in school. If so, he didn't retain any of it. But it was all moot. He wasn't healthy—he was missing a leg.

A tear rolled down his cheek. He was on the track team in high school. Why, oh why, didn't he say no to exploring the building? He had the perfect excuse—they wanted him to work. But exploring the building was cooler. Stupid!

Nothing he could do about it now. He had no way to make it home, and he knew no one. Maybe it would be better if he died.

"Pete?"

He turned his head at the sound of the voice. It was familiar to him. Oh, so familiar.

She was looking down at him. She was wearing the outfit of an ambulance driver. That couldn't be.

But it was.

"Barbara?"

Chapter 34

AT SEA—1918

As Barbara sat on a troop ship headed for Europe, she didn't once doubt her decision to leave Alice and the others. Pete was out there someplace alone. He might be with other soldiers, but he was essentially alone. It couldn't end like this for him.

Barbara had made a few friends among the other women. Most of them had boyfriends who were fighting. There was always the hope that they would be assigned somewhere close to their boyfriends. So, when Barbara said that she was following Pete, the others understood.

"I'm told that the chances of seeing my boyfriend Mike are slim," said Mary, who had become Barbara's closest friend in the group. "But I've gotta try. Besides, what we're doing is important."

There were over a hundred women on the ship—a hundred women to perform the difficult and dangerous jobs of nurses, ambulance drivers, and technicians. All but Barbara had signed up for patriotic reasons. Working near their boyfriend or husband was a perk if it could happen, but mostly, they were there for their country. Barbara, however, was going for only one reason—to find Pete.

Barbara tried to stay on deck as much as possible, as it was stuffy and generally unhealthy below. If one woman caught a cold, they all had it hours later. It could be chilly up on deck, but Barbara loved looking out at the ocean. The sea was rough, and Barbara had to hold on tight, but it was still better than being down below. It also smelled down there—many of the women became sick from the rough seas. The space for the women was small, as most of the ship was taken up by the troops.

Food was plentiful, but little of it was eaten with the seas so rough.

When they finally reached the shores of France, they couldn't wait to disembark. Once ashore, they were quickly grouped by their assigned jobs. Within hours, Barbara was on her way to a place she had never heard of, but where the fighting was fierce. They had ambulances, but not enough drivers. Barbara's friend, Mary, also an ambulance driver, was at Barbara's side for the long trip to the front.

"Are you scared?" asked Mary.

"I guess," answered Barbara. "Are you?"

"I'm scared, but we can't let the Huns win."

"They won't," answered Barbara without thinking.

"How can you say that so knowingly?"

"I have confidence," replied Barbara, fixing her mistake. After hearing what happened to Pete when he tried to tell people he was from the future, she was usually careful in what she said. Coming out to Ruth and Bill was easy since they held the upper hand. Bill and Ruth had no choice but to listen to them. With Pete, it was different.

Barbara heard gunfire in the distance, but it was getting louder as the troop truck maneuvered the potholes in the muddy road. They were close now.

They arrived at their destination an hour later. The women were given a crash course in where to go and where not to go in their ambulances and were put to work as soon as their gear was stowed in their tents.

A few months earlier, Barbara was attending classes at Harvard. Now, she was in the middle of a brutal war.

All because she entered a time portal that no one even knew existed.

*****

She'd been there two months and had seen more blood than she'd ever imagined. The cries of the wounded were the worst part. Growing up, Barbara had been in the hospital a few times. This was nothing like her experiences. She had been in several areas of fighting, and in each one, the hospital was rudimentary at best—nothing more than a large tent with dozens of cots. The hospitals were crowded, bloody, and depressing places. There was never enough room for the wounded. The doctors and nurses worked around the clock and were in a perpetual state of exhaustion.

Barbara began to forget that World War One had already happened. It was just numbers in the history books. But these weren't numbers. These men were flesh and blood—with an emphasis on the blood. Yes, maybe where she came from, World War One had already happened, but she was living it now. When she comforted a soldier, she wasn't comforting a historical statistic. She was comforting a scared real-life person.

She wasn't particularly religious, but Barbara couldn't help thinking that going through the portal must have happened for a reason. Then again, maybe it was all just wild chance. Maybe there was no rhyme or reason to anything. Maybe it was just chaos at work.

Barbara had lost her friend Mary two weeks earlier when Mary's ambulance took a direct hit from a mortar. Her death hit

Barbara hard, but there was no time for mourning. The job was all-consuming, and all feelings had to be pushed down in order to keep moving on.

Barbara moved as the front lines moved, with no sense of stability. Wherever she went, though, Barbara kept an eye out for Pete. She checked rosters, lists of the dead and wounded, and if the opportunity came up, she would ask platoon leaders. She found three Peter Greens, but none were her Peter.

Then, one day, by chance, a nurse approached her. Barbara had just been transferred to another battle zone.

"Are you the one looking for Peter Green?"

"Yes, I am," said Barbara, a lump appearing in her throat.

"I accompanied one in an ambulance two days ago. He had been severely wounded. I don't know if he's the one you are looking for, but he's in the hospital."

"Thank you!" said Barbara. "I'll see if it's him."

"I must warn you that he's in rough shape. The doctors are worried about blood poisoning. He has bad wounds." She hesitated. "He also lost a leg."

"Oh no!" Barbara covered her mouth with her hands.

"I thought you should know."

Having seen what she had in the two months, Barbara recovered quickly. She gave the nurse a quick hug.

"Thank you for telling me. And thank you for caring for him, whether or not it's my Pete."

*****

Now, as she stood over her lover, it took everything she had not to cry. Pete was almost unrecognizable—a bloody bandaged stump where his leg used to be, bloody bandages around his chest and abdomen, and stitches above his eye that had been hastily administered.

"Is it really you?"

He had tears in his eyes.

Barbara leaned down and gently hugged him.

"It's me. I can't believe I found you. Do you have any idea how many Peter Greens there are in the Army?"

"What are you doing here?"

"I joined the ambulance corps to try to find you."

"So, you came through the portal, too?"

He began to cough, leading to a full-blown coughing fit. It sounded like pneumonia to Barbara. That wasn't good. She gave him a sip of water.

"We all went through. For some reason, Nicholas suggested we hold hands, so we all went through together and landed in the same time. We arrived a few months after you."

"Did you meet the nasty people who owned the place?" Pete's voice was barely above a whisper now.

"We did. We stayed with them. We convinced them we were from the future. Pete, they feel horrible about the way they treated you. They were scared."

"I hope they go to hell," said Pete.

Barbara didn't say anything. She understood. He wouldn't be here dying if it hadn't been for them.

Dying! Barbara didn't know why she thought that—but at the same time, she did know. In her two months on the line, she had seen a lot of death, and many of the boys died of wounds less severe than Pete's. Now it sounded like pneumonia had set in from his chest wounds. She wanted to cry but couldn't—not in front of him.

"Barbara, c'mon." A nurse stood at the door of the massive tent, motioning to her. It was the nurse on Barbara's ambulance. "We need to make another run, quick. The fighting has intensified."

"I'll be right there," replied Barbara.

"Go," said Pete. "I'll be fine. You have a job to do. Just be careful."

"I will," said Barbara, kissing him lightly on the lips.

"And Barbara,"

"Yes?"

"Thank you for coming after me. Even if I die tomorrow, you've brought me so much joy. I'm just sorry I got us into this mess."

"It wasn't your fault," said Barbara. "We all made the decision." The nurse was waving to her. "Look, I have to go. They won't send me on another one after this today, so as soon as I get back, I'll sit with you, and we can talk. I love you."

"I love you, too."

Barbara hurried out of the tent to start her next run.

Due to the intensity of the fighting and the number of wounded, they did add a second run to her schedule. It was a grueling day, and she was exhausted by the time her shift was over.

She had to see Pete before she crashed for the night. It was late evening by the time she made it back to him—but there was another man in Pete's bunk. She caught the arm of a doctor.

"Doctor, can you tell me what happened to Peter Green, who occupied this bunk?"

The doctor gave a tired sigh and checked his list.

"Private Green died earlier this afternoon." Looking at her expression, he added, "Was he special to you?"

She nodded, the tears creating streaks through the dirt on her face.

"I'm sorry. His wounds were just too great."

"Thank you," she said quietly, touching the doctor's arm.

*****

Barbara shut down after that. She did her job, even asking for extra shifts to dampen her feelings of loss. She went out of her way to avoid making friends. It wasn't worth it. After all, they would just die. She had come for Pete, and now he wasn't there. Alice and the others were probably through the portal to 1950, so she was all alone.

Two weeks later, her ambulance took a direct hit from a mortar shell. The nurse and technician on board were immediately killed, as were the patients.

As Barbara lay by the side of the road bleeding, she reached a hand up.

"Pete."

And then she took her final breath.

PART THREE

Chapter 35

FREMONT, NEBRASKA—1950

Hanna pulled her weapon from her backpack.

"What do you mean that someone has to die?" asked Alex.

"You're going to kill someone right here on the street?" asked Randy, shocked at what he had just heard.

"Of course not," replied Hanna. "I'll follow him and find a secluded spot."

"Can you explain what's going on?" asked Alex.

"Remember the note from Ray, where he mentioned the fugitive from my time having hooked up with some accidental travelers? His name is Nicholas Gates."

"Right. He's a mass murderer."

"Exactly." For Randy's benefit, she explained, "He killed more than thirty employees of a humanitarian organization."

"Whoa!" said Randy.

"That's him across the street. I saw his picture so many times over the year before we left, I'd never forget his face, his body, and the way he walks. There is no doubt in my mind that he's Gates. We can't have him roaming through time. He has to be stopped. The two he's with must be two of the innocent travelers from 2026. There should be one or two more, but I don't see them."

"They look out of place," said Randy.

"Very out of place," said Hanna. "They're all wearing brand new clothes. They probably came through the same portal we did. Maybe we can help them after I take care of Gates."

They followed Gates and the other two down Main Street until they reached a hotel. Gates and the others went in.

"That's good," said Hanna. "It'll be easy to get him."

"I think this is the hotel we were directed to. We should check in there," said Alex. "After you do what you need to do, maybe we can help the others. Since we need a place to stay tonight, it may as well be here. I'll go in and get us two rooms."

Randy just shook his head.

"You'll get a room in the same place you're going to kill someone? That's ballsy."

Hanna just shrugged. She had been in similar situations numerous times and had become hardened to them.

When Alex walked in, Gates and the others were still at the counter finalizing their rooms for the night. Alex heard enough to get their names, Keith and Alice Miller, and the room number. Nicholas Gates used his real name and had a room across the hall from the Millers.

When the trio had gone up the stairs, Alex secured a room for him and Hanna and another for Randy. As the hotel only had two levels, they were put on the second floor, the same floor as the threesome they were following. Once he had the keys, Alex went back outside.

"Nicholas Gates is using his real name," he said.

"To be expected," said Hanna, "he's not an experienced time traveler. He doesn't know the rules about changing your name."

"We're right down the hall from them. Apropos of nothing, the other two checked in as a married couple, but I don't think they are married. I think they were just thrown together."

"I'm not surprised," replied Hanna. "It's probably the only

way they can stay sane. Besides, we always check in places as a married couple, so it's also the easier way to do things."

"Maybe we can take them with us to the next portal—the one that brings them out in 2030," said Randy.

"If it really does," said Hanna. "But it's a good idea. First, though, I have to kill Gates."

"You say that so casually," said Randy.

"Maybe," replied Hanna, "but there is nothing casual about it."

"As someone who was misunderstood," said Randy, "can I suggest stunning him first, and giving him the opportunity to present his side of the story? What if he's innocent?"

"You make a good point," said Hanna. "In all the news reports, he said that it was something that had to be done. Maybe there's something here that we're missing. However, I'm not giving him too much rope."

Their opportunity to confront Gates came a few minutes later as they reached their floor. Gates and the Millers were standing in the hallway, discussing something.

"Excuse me," said Hanna, "we're new to Fremont. Do you know a good place to eat?"

"I'm afraid we're new, too," said Keith. "Your best bet is to ask—"

Hanna lifted her arm, revealing the weapon in her hand. Nicholas stiffened. Set for area stun, she pulled the trigger, and the three dropped to the floor.

"We have to move fast," she said. "The area stun doesn't last long at all."

They pulled the three unconscious people into the room with the open door they had been standing outside of. Using Nicholas's own belt, Alex tied his hands behind his back and sat him on the floor, leaning against the bed. They didn't bother tying the other two. They carried them to the bed.

A few minutes later, all three opened their eyes. The two on the bed seemed frightened—Nicholas was calm and collected, as if being tied up was a regular occurrence.

Nobody said anything at first.

Finally, Alex addressed Keith and Alice.

"We're sorry we had to stun you. You weren't our target, but it was easier this way. My name is Alex. This is Hanna, and the other gentleman is Randy. You are Nicholas Gates," he said to Nicholas, "and you two are—"

"Keith and Alice Miller," said Keith hurriedly.

"Well, I know you're not really married," said Hanna, "but it doesn't matter. You look happy together, especially considering all that you've probably gone through."

"How—" started Keith.

"How do we know what you've been through?" asked Hanna. "Because we've got you beat. You haven't even begun to know the troubles that time travel brings. But we'll talk to you about that later. My question is for Gates. Give me a good reason not to kill you."

"You have me at a loss," said Nicholas calmly. "Who are you, and why do you want to kill me?"

"Does the year 2104 mean anything to you?" asked Hanna.

"The fact that you're asking means that you know it does. Are you part of the Time Travel Project, or some sort of cop from that time?"

"I *was* part of the Time Travel Project," said Hanna, "but it doesn't exist anymore."

"So, all you know is what you heard on the news at the time."

"It was enough."

"But it wasn't the truth."

"Can someone explain what's happening?" asked Keith. To Nicholas, he said, "Are you a time traveler? Have you been lying to us all these months?"

"Kind of, and no, I haven't been lying. I just haven't told you anything—there's a difference."

"Not much of one."

"In 2104," Hanna said to Keith and Alice, "Nicholas Gates was convicted of slaughtering over thirty members of a humanitarian organization. He went to prison but escaped soon after." She turned to Nicholas. "Do you deny it?"

"I don't deny escaping from prison," said Nicholas. "And I don't deny slaughtering over thirty people. But I take issue with the term, 'humanitarian organization.'"

"What do you mean?" asked Alex.

"There was nothing humanitarian about them."

Chapter 36

WASHINGTON DC—2104

What did he get himself into now?

It was supposed to be a simple job—one that he could do in his sleep. His bosses were being kind to him as he approached retirement. All he had to do was follow an arms dealer named Franklin and see who he met. And Nicholas already knew who the man was going to meet with—an influential city council member who had a beef with the other council members. Supposedly, the council member was out to settle the score the old-fashioned way—blow the others up. At least, that was the information they had received.

Nicholas knew Franklin, the arms dealer. Not the sharpest knife in the drawer, but competent at his job. He had inherited the business from his father, one of the most successful arms dealers in the world—that is, until he was blown up by his own product. Rumor had it that Franklin was involved, but it was just a rumor. It didn't matter. This was just a routine meeting for Franklin, and a lightweight assignment for Nicholas.

Nicholas was once the top Interpol agent in the world. No assignment was too difficult. He had better than a 90 percent success rate, which was phenomenal considering the difficulty of his assignments—assignments that no one else would touch.

He was getting old now. Fifty-six wasn't old by most standards, but it was almost ancient in his line of work. He was taking on a few low-key jobs until his retirement in a few months. He was ready. Besides, the people at the top were all different. In just the last year, the directorship and many of the other higher-level jobs had been taken over by people who lacked the vision of Interpol.

Once an international police force connected to police forces worldwide, Interpol became an independent entity thirty years earlier, just as Nicholas was hired. Being independent gave them more power to do as they saw fit, including crossing the line when necessary. But it pissed off the international community, who no longer had input. Interpol was now on the same level as the NSA, CIA, Mossad, and others.

And Nicholas Gates was its star.

But the new leadership bothered him. They were secretive and unreachable.

Yes, it was time to retire.

Nicholas stood behind an overflowing dumpster and took pictures of Franklin waiting to meet the city councilman. The man had chosen to walk, which was fine with Nicholas. In this day of flying cars, it was more difficult to follow someone and obtain substantive information. Nicholas liked the old-fashioned way and missed the days when everything was confined to the ground.

Another good reason to retire.

It was happening. A car descended and landed next to the arms dealer. Two men got out. One was the city councilman. Who was the other?

Suddenly, Nicholas recognized him. James Stout, head of the humanitarian organization Future Save. What the hell was he doing there?

It looked like the councilman was introducing Stout to

Franklin.

Franklin pulled a small device from his coat. Even from that distance, Nicholas knew what it was—a portable remote detonator. He had seen enough of them over the years. Why would the head of a humanitarian organization need a detonator?

Stout handed the arms dealer a bag. It had to be the payoff. Stout then got back into the car with the councilman. The car ascended and joined the wall-to-wall traffic that filled the sky.

Everything had changed. It was no longer a simple operation to confirm the councilman's murderous intent. This was new and different. His instructions were to let the arms dealer walk. Not now. He was making new instructions.

The arms dealer walked back toward Nicholas, intending to walk along the river to his boat.

"Hello, Franklin," said Nicholas, stepping out from behind the dumpster.

The man stopped in his tracks. Nicholas could see his mind working, trying to figure a way out of the situation.

"You can see from there that the weapon in my hand is set to stun. You may think that's good, but it's really not. Because when you wake up, the things I'm going to do to you will make you wish I had killed you."

"Hi, Gates." The man was trying to be cool but was sweating profusely. There was nothing cool about him. "Why the threats? What did I ever do to you?"

"To me? Nothing. To thousands of dead people around the world? Plenty. I had orders to let you walk, and I might still follow them if you give me the information I'm looking for."

"Such as?"

"Why were you meeting with James Stout? I understood that you were meeting with that rat of a city councilman."

"Things changed. I made a lot more money doing this, as did the rat of a councilman. So, he changed his plans."

"What were you doing for Stout?"

"You know I can't tell you that."

"How about I let you keep the payoff and be on your merry way in exchange for the information? Franklin, I'm going to get the information from you one way or another. Don't be stupid. What have you got to lose? You already have your money."

Franklin considered it, then said, "Okay, you win. This was a big job. I didn't just sell him the arms; I oversaw their placement."

"Placement of what?"

"Nuclear devices—lots of small nuclear devices."

"Where?"

"India. Enough to wipe out most of the big cities."

"That's crazy. Why would he do that? He's the head of a humanitarian organization."

"And what's the name of the organization? Future Save. He's trying to save the future by reducing the world's population. India has some of the worst conditions in the world. He wipes out the cities, waits a few years for the dust to settle, and then the world repopulates it from other overcrowded countries and continents. A fresh start."

"Who in his organization is involved in this?"

"Who? Everyone. He was very careful to pick people who would do his bidding."

"The whole organization?"

"Think about it. How hard would it be to get people to work with you who had the same vision of the future? You have to make sacrifices. The whole world is a garbage pit. So, you wipe out the worst areas and start over. You move people from overcrowded areas into this new empty land. The word I get is that this is only the first. He has other targets in mind."

"When is he doing this?"

"Tomorrow at the latest. It's all set up. All he has to do is type the code into the detonator."

"I guess I have to move fast."

"And do what?" asked Franklin. "Go to your people? Who do you think is behind all this?"

"Interpol?"

"Well, not Interpol, the organization, but the head people. This has been a long time coming. I can't believe the Golden Boy, Nicholas Gates, hasn't gotten wind of it. In my business, we all know about it. You just happened to stumble on it because the councilman made the mistake of being seen with Stout tonight. I'm sure your people at the top had no idea that Stout had enlisted the services of such an idiot as the councilman."

"How sure are you that my bosses at Interpol are behind this?"

"Check it out yourself. I know your reputation. In the past, if you informed them that something was going down immediately, you'd get the clearance to do whatever you had to do to stop it, right?"

Nicholas nodded.

"So, contact them now. Let them know what's happening. I guarantee that they'll tell you to sit on it or send it up through the proper channels, which will take days at the very least. Just understand something. The minute you do that, you put a target on your back. This is too important to them. You will be marked for termination. Drop it now, or you're a dead man. I guarantee it."

Nicholas had heard enough. He was tired—tired of the job, tired of the scumbags he had to deal with, tired of not making a difference. After all, had the world improved in the thirty years he'd done his job? Of course not. Well, he could make a difference starting now.

He flicked his weapon to "kill." Franklin saw the move, and his eyes got wide.

"We had a deal—"

Nicholas's shot got Franklin in the middle of the forehead. He dropped to the ground. Nicholas picked up the bag of money and walked three blocks to a large soup kitchen. He walked in and was directed to the manager's office, where a harried woman sat at a desk poring over pages of figures.

"Here, this might help," he said, dropping the bag on the desk. He then turned and left before the woman could say anything.

Once outside, he called his office and got his new supervisor, an assistant director. He explained what was happening and that they needed to work quickly before a major catastrophe occurred.

"Are you sure?" asked the supervisor.

"Absolutely."

"We'll have to take this under advisement."

"We don't have time," said Nicholas. "You know my reputation within the organization. If I say it's imminent, it's imminent. They've never needed to take it under advisement before. My word was always good enough."

"Things have changed. Why don't you come on in? We can discuss it."

Nicholas knew what that meant. But he couldn't let them think he was going to do anything on his own, so he said, "Okay. I think it's a bad idea, but I'll be right in."

He hung up.

So, that was how it was going to be.

He had only one choice left.

Chapter 37

FREMONT, NEBRASKA—1950

"I did what I had to do," said Nicholas. "I accessed the Future Save's employee list—"

"How?" interrupted Keith.

"How? That kind of information was available everywhere."

Nicholas looked to Hanna for confirmation.

"It's true," she said. "There was very little the average person couldn't get if they had the know-how. And most people had the know-how."

"I went to the Future Save offices," continued Nicholas. "Most of the employees were still working even though it was night, which told me something big was going down. I killed them all. I know that those of you from the late 20th or early 21st century will find that shocking, but you had to know the times."

"It was still shocking," said Hanna, "even then."

"Then you had to understand my business. We did what had to be done. Anyway, James Stout and his assistant director weren't in their offices. I tracked them down at their homes and killed them. Then I destroyed the detonator, making the nuclear devices useless."

"Maybe I'm just slow," said Hanna, "but didn't they do away

with nuclear weapons late in the 21st century?"

"They did away with them, but it doesn't mean they destroyed them. This group got their hands on dozens of small nuclear devices. They had a master plan for eradicating millions—maybe billions of people, to reduce the population of the Earth."

"Why India, specifically?" asked Alex.

"It had to be a country they worked in on a humanitarian basis—well, a fake humanitarian basis. They also wanted countries that were poor and way behind the rest of the world technologically. India was once one of the most technically advanced countries, but the overpopulation was too much to overcome. As a result, they lost their edge. Future Save's idea was that once it was safe again to repopulate those areas, people from other continents would relocate there, helping to ease overpopulation worldwide. If they started with India, what country would be next?"

"Besides the obvious reason of mass extinction, there are so many other things wrong with that plan," said Alex.

"Exactly," said Nicholas.

"Was the world dangerously overcrowded?" asked Alice.

"It was," answered Hanna, "and very little was being done about it. However, mass extinction wasn't the answer."

"It wasn't," said Nicholas. "Anyway, my own organization arrested me and sent me to prison."

"Why didn't they just kill you?" asked Randy.

"They needed a scapegoat. Sending me to prison solved it."

"Why didn't you say anything?" asked Hanna. "I watched the newscasts. All you said was that they needed to die."

"It would have done no good. No one would believe it. Their best plan was to send me to prison. There was no doubt in my mind that once in prison, I wouldn't last a week before they had me killed. So, I escaped. I knew about the Time Travel Project. It was a secret to the rest of the world, but not to the NSA or some of us in Interpol. I also knew there was a portal in the basement of the Time Travel Project headquarters, so I stole a Portal Finder and used the portal."

"How did you escape?" asked Randy.

"A story for another time. It's what I'm good at."

"So, you were like a spy," said Keith.

"Pretty much."

"You don't look the part," said Alice.

"You mean ruggedly handsome?"

"Sorry. I didn't mean it like that."

"No, you're right. But looking like this gets me into places I wouldn't be able to if I looked the stereotypical part."

Hanna looked at Alex, who shrugged. Was he telling the truth? It seemed too elaborate to be made up.

"What are you doing here?" asked Alex.

"I came back in time for two reasons—to escape that time, and to hunt down the ancestors of the people at the top of Interpol. If I could get rid of the gene pool, maybe none of that would've happened, and I wouldn't be put in the situation I was."

"Well, you can forget about the second part of your plan," said Hanna, "because it doesn't work that way. We've determined that you can't change history—at least not in the way you mean. You're talking about wiping out memories and experiences, and that's not possible. If an event happened, you can't wipe it out. If it happened, it happened. Once someone experiences it and has it imprinted in their memory, you can't take it away from them."

"You're sure?"

"We're sure. We've experienced it. It can't happen."

"I wondered about that. So, the scientists of the time had it all wrong."

"It was all theory," said Hanna. "They had no conclusive evidence. They could only surmise."

"Ray Burton warned us of that possibility in his last

communication. So, I guess I'm just on the run and without a purpose."

"I remember you reacting to something in his note," said Keith. "That was it, wasn't it?"

"It was. It was the first I had heard that we couldn't change history."

"Something I don't understand," said Keith, "is why you chose to join my group."

"That's easy," said Nicholas. "I guess I can tell you now."

He paused.

"Because you were my first target."

Chapter 38

"Me?"

"One of your descendants becomes the head of Interpol."

"How do you know that?" asked Alex.

"People's ancestry was all accessible. It took me less than an hour to download everything I needed after I escaped. I landed in 2010, which is where that portal took me. I could have started my search from there, but they were on my trail. They sent someone after me, so I had to keep moving. I took a portal in Arizona that was supposed to send me back to 1870, but it sent me to 2026 instead. I don't know how that happened."

Hanna decided not to tell Nicholas about the portals shifting until she knew whether or not he was lying. Alex followed her lead.

"Once I was there," continued Nicholas, "you were the most accessible of my targets. I was going to kill you immediately, but then I read that you were taking a group to North Conway to explore an abandoned building. I knew there was a portal somewhere up there. I figured I could kill you and escape through the portal. When we arrived, I looked at my Portal Finder and saw that it was in the building we were exploring. It was a fortuitous development. Kill you and escape within minutes."

"Why didn't you?" asked Keith.

"I had doubts. You seemed like a good person. I may have been capable and experienced at killing, but it suddenly didn't seem right. In fact, I was having second thoughts about my whole mission. Now that you've told me I can't change history, I know I made the right decision."

"Wait a minute," said Alice. "Were you responsible for Pete falling into the portal? Did you cut his rope?"

"He fell in on his own—strictly an accident. No one cut his rope—the portal did. I assume that the part of his rope that went into the portal went with him."

"Yes, that would make sense," said Hanna.

"Wait," said Keith. "You've had a Portal Finder all this time?"

"No. When Pete fell, his rope pulled me to my knees. I hadn't latched my backpack. When I went to my knees, I was bent over. The Portal finder was in the top of my backpack, and it fell out into a hole."

"The portal?" asked Keith.

"No, just a hole in the building. I planned to retrieve it, but then we entered the portal, and that ended that."

"It's probably under a ton of dirt right now," said Keith.

"Hold on," said Alice. "If you knew where the portal was and you had already decided not to kill Keith, why didn't you warn us? Why did you make us go through it with you? You could have gone by yourself."

"I tried, remember? I attempted to go first, but Keith wouldn't let me. I figured that if I went through and disappeared, you'd know it was a portal and wouldn't follow. So, when Keith insisted on going first, the best I could do was to make sure we all arrived together. In retrospect, I would have done it differently. I might have held you all at gunpoint and gone through alone. It all happened too quickly. Look, it was a mistake on my part—a big mistake. Ten years ago—hell, five years ago—I wouldn't have made that mistake. I would have made a split-second decision, and it would have been the right one. The fact is, I'm slowing down. My choice of a career has taken its toll after all these years. I guess mentally, I'm not where I once was. All I can say is that I regret the decision. It ruined your lives and I'm sorry."

There was nothing any of them could say. Hanna thought that he seemed genuine in his regret.

"Can I ask you a question?" Nicholas asked Hanna.

Hanna nodded.

"If I can't change history, what would happen if I killed someone?"

"It's a question we have grappled with," replied Hanna. "Based on the experience of Alex's grandfather getting killed, all we can guess is that it's an alternate history of some kind. Alex saw him die, yet it didn't change any of the memories Alex had of him. In that experience, his wife mourned his death, yet Alex has memories of them together years later. So, 'alternate history' is the best explanation we can come up with."

"Nicholas mentioned your descendants. You're going to have children," Alice said to Keith. "Does that mean you get back to Cyndi?"

"I don't know what it means. I just know that I came close to dying."

"And I apologize for my intentions," said Nicholas, "you have nothing to worry about from me."

"Good to know."

"Speaking of intentions," said Nicholas, "what are your plans for me? I've been completely honest with you."

Alex and Hanna looked at each other. It was a good question. What to do with Nicholas? Alex thought his story seemed plausible, and he didn't have the demeanor of a mass murderer—whatever that might be. But what if they were wrong?

"If I can add my two cents," said Keith, "despite his earlier intentions that I knew nothing about, we've spent months with

Nicholas and have never felt threatened. We always felt that there was something odd about him—and knew that there was something he was hiding—but we never felt threatened. And I believe his story."

Hanna touched Alex's arm, confirming what Alex was thinking. He walked over to Nicholas and told him to stand up and turn around so he could take the belt off his wrists. Nicholas held up his hands. There was no belt.

"I took it off while I talked," said Nicholas. "As I said, I'm good at what I do. But in all honesty, this wasn't very hard. You really must work on your belt-tying skills."

Alex flashed him a slight smile, then sat down. For a full minute, there was an uncomfortable silence in the room.

"So, are we okay?" Nicholas finally asked.

"I guess we are," answered Hanna. "You're welcome to accompany us—you all are. We are heading to a portal that supposedly takes us to 2030."

Keith and Alice glanced at each other. The glance had a meaning, but Hanna couldn't guess what it was.

"We were about to check the Portal Finder Ray Burton sent us. That date probably would have come up. But why did you use the word 'supposedly' when you gave the date?" Keith asked.

"Because it's no longer a guarantee that the date you see on the Portal Finder will be the one you go to," answered Hanna. "Just as Nicholas experienced with the Hollow Rock, Arizona, portal. I'll explain it later. Meanwhile, let's get to know each other. We were under the impression that there were more of you."

They spent the next hour discussing their lives. The only one who opted out was Nicholas. Alex had no doubt that there was a lot of darkness in his past—darkness that he probably wanted to forget. When Keith and Alice told them about meeting and falling in love, Hanna pinpointed the problem.

"When I mentioned the year 2030, you gave each other a sad

glance. I think I know why. If you arrive four years after you left, it will mean the end of your relationship. Cyndi will still be there, and you'll still be married, Keith."

"Yes," acknowledged Keith. "Please don't misunderstand. I love Cyndi, and Alice understands that. But I also love Alice and am loving her more deeply every day." He took Alice's hand. "So yes, it's hard. I'm not sure what I'm going to do. I have the best of both worlds, and the worst of both worlds. I just have a feeling that, at this point, I'm not going to be able to go back to Cyndi, and that's not fair to her."

"Or by then, maybe she will have moved on," said Alex.

"The only advice I can give you is to wait and see what happens," said Hanna. "We might get to the next portal and find that it died. Dilemma solved."

It wasn't enough to cheer up Keith and Alice, however.

They arranged to meet at dinnertime and find a place to eat. In the meantime, they all retreated to their rooms.

"Keith is hurting," said Hanna.

They rested on the bed, absorbing all they had learned about Nicholas and the others.

"It's guilt," said Alex. "He feels like he's betrayed Cyndi. He knows that he needs to get on with his life and is happy to have found Alice, but he's also harboring deep guilt. I think the only way it will be solved is if they are unable to make it home. So, the worst-case scenario is also the best. I feel for him."

"I'm glad you weren't in that situation when we met," said Hanna.

"Ha. The woman I was dating probably forgot my name a week after I disappeared."

"Well, good," said Hanna, snuggling up to him.

*****

They all met in the hallway at 5:00.

"You grew up in this time period, so you're familiar with it," Hanna said to Alex. "What are we looking for?"

"It doesn't really matter," he replied. "Whatever we find will be better than the food any of us are used to—especially you, Nicholas, from what I hear about food in the 22nd century. Everything here is fresh."

They found a family restaurant a block away, in the center of town. Halfway into their meal, they all admitted that Alex wasn't exaggerating.

"Are you sure we want to go home?" Keith asked Alice. "I could eat this food every night."

"I never said I wanted to go home," said Alice. "I just want to be with you."

"Hey, this is a family restaurant," said Randy with a laugh. "Save that stuff for your room."

Everyone laughed except Nicholas, who was staring over several empty tables to the street beyond.

"You okay?" asked Hanna.

"No."

He slid his .45 out from behind his back and his silencer from his pocket. As he screwed on the silencer, he said, "No one look, but there is a man across the street watching us. He might be one of the people coming after me."

Randy asked Hanna, "Could he be one of those Eliminators you talked about?"

"Maybe, but to our knowledge, none of them are left. My guess is that Nicholas is right—they are on a mission to get him. How many did they send back after you?"

"I have no idea," said Nicholas, "but I'm sure they were concerned about me going on a murder spree and changing history."

"Little did they know that you probably wouldn't have

changed history even if you went on your spree," said Alex.

"Yeah, well, I feel a little murderous right now," replied Nicholas. "Wait here."

Nicholas got up and headed for the bathroom in the back. He opened the Men's Room door, took a quick look, and was satisfied with what he saw—a large window. If the bathroom had a small window—or no window—he would have had to go out through the kitchen to the back door. That would bring attention to the group, which was the last thing he wanted.

Nicholas had grown fond of Keith and Alice but knew his time with them was ending. If there really were people coming after him from the 22nd century, he couldn't put the two of them in constant danger. After he took care of this business, maybe it was time to move on. He'd steal the Portal Finder from his intended assassin and be on his way.

First things first, though.

He had to take care of the assassin.

Nicholas tried the window. It opened easily and just high enough for him to squeeze through. It led to an alley running along the side of the restaurant. He landed quietly and looked around to make sure he was alone.

It was dusk, and Nicholas had on dark clothes. Hopefully, he would blend in before the man saw him. He reached the end of the alley and carefully looked around the corner.

The man was gone!

"Shit," Nicholas mumbled under his breath.

Something hit him in the side, and he slid down the wall into a sitting position. Right where his head had been a moment earlier, the brick exploded. His wound had saved him from certain death. The pain in his side was intense, but Nicholas knew he had to move. He got to his knees and was stopped by a voice.

"You may as well accept your fate. You're going to die tonight.

"What did I ever do to you?" asked Nicholas.

"Nothing. Nothing at all. It's what I'm going to get out of it."

"And what's that?"

"Money. Lots of money."

"Indulge me before you shoot me. Who's paying you, and how?"

"No, I don't think I will indulge you."

The man lifted his weapon.

Nicholas had his .45 by his leg, resting on the ground, and had lifted the barrel slightly. He pulled the trigger, and the silenced round shot out of the gun. But just as he shot, the man turned and dropped to the ground. Nicholas's bullet went through the man's backpack.

Hanna came around the corner with her weapon extended.

"I set it for stun in case you wanted to interrogate him," she said.

"Thank you," he replied, wheezing as he talked. "I was going to have to kill him, and I really didn't want to."

"You're hurt!" cried Alice.

The others had joined Hanna.

"I don't think it's serious," said Nicholas. "I think he creased my side."

He looked around.

"We have to get out of here. People are going to be curious."

So far, no one had come by, but that wouldn't last.

"Help me pick this guy up," Alex said to Keith. "He's now a friend who had too much to drink, and we're bringing him back to the hotel. Nicholas, can you walk on your own?"

"For the most part. Randy can help me if I need it. We should use the back door of the hotel. Hanna and Alice should go in the front entrance."

Alex knew that Hanna would be upset to be used as a diversion, instead of being in the thick of things, but she'd get over it once she was able to interrogate the prisoner.

With the hotel only a block away, they made it back without drawing too much attention. They had to use the "drunk" excuse once, but it seemed to satisfy the worried questioner. Twenty minutes after the incident in the alley, they were all in Nicholas's room.

"Let's see what he has to say," said Hanna.

Chapter 39

Alex tied up Nicholas's attacker—this time doing a better job with the belt—while Keith looked at Nicholas's wound.

"You're lucky," said Keith, "it just went through the outer layer and missed anything vital."

"Are you a medic?" asked Nicholas.

"EMT," said Keith. "I was trying to get into paramedic school, but I guess that's not going to happen. However, I can take care of this."

"Do you need anything?" asked Hanna. "I can run out to the store."

"I saw a drugstore on the next block," said Keith. He quickly wrote down a list of items he needed, and Hanna left to get them.

"Don't start without me," she said as she went through the door,

She returned in fifteen minutes with everything Keith wanted, including antiseptic, bandages, and a needle and thread. Meanwhile, the assassin still slept.

Their prisoner woke up about the same time Keith finished the patch job on Nicholas.

"Who are you people?" asked the man.

He looked to be in his late thirties, but Alex thought he might have been younger. He looked like someone who had led a hard life, but then, it seemed that no one from the 22nd century enjoyed an easy life. His hair was black and messy, and he had a few days' beard growth.

"We'll be your worst nightmare if you don't answer our questions," said Alex. "If you satisfy us with your answers, maybe we'll let you go."

"Maybe?"

"It'll be up to you. So, who are you?"

"My name is George."

"Okay, George, why were you trying to kill Nicholas?"

"Do you know who he is?"

"We do."

"Then you know why I'm here."

"Explain it to us anyway. I assume you are from the year 2105?"

"Why do you assume that?"

"It's the year the Time Travel Project began, and a year after Nicholas killed all those people. It makes sense."

"Not to me, it doesn't," said George. "I'm from 2116."

At their puzzled expressions, he continued, "Yes, he slaughtered those people in 2104, but it wasn't until 2116 that they hired people to go after him."

"Why?" asked Hanna.

"I can't answer that because I don't know. They wouldn't tell us."

"Who is 'they,' and 'us?'" asked Alex.

"Interpol. They hired a bunch of us—I don't know how many. We never saw each other. Money was transferred into our accounts. The one who killed Gates was promised a $5 million bonus."

"I still don't get why they waited so long to send people back after him," said Hanna.

"We weren't told anything except that he killed those people.

They said they couldn't chase him before, but now they can. We can follow him. They said we had to get him because he could change the future. All of us might cease to exist."

Alex looked at Hanna. Something wasn't adding up.

And then Hanna realized what George was talking about.

"Of course," she said. "You're from 2116. That explains it."

"I don't know what you're talking about, lady."

Nicholas slapped him hard across the cheek.

"Let's show some manners."

"How were you getting home?" asked Hanna.

"They gave me something called a Portal Finder. I tracked Gates with it. They said I could use it to get home."

"Maybe," said Hanna.

"What do you mean by maybe?"

"You've been lied to, but more on that later. So, let me get this straight: You and others were hired to travel back in time and kill Nicholas, and then find your way home, right?"

"Right."

"You were all paid to do it, and the one who killed him would get a $5 million bonus."

"Right."

"I'm not understanding this," said Nicholas. "How can he track me?"

"It's all making sense now," replied Hanna. "Nicholas, your Interpol buddies were under the same misconception that you were—that you could significantly change history. Did you tell anyone your plan?"

"The only person I told was the Time Travel Project person I tied up. I did it for a reason. I wanted the people responsible for this to spend the rest of their lives wondering if they would just disappear one day. Even if I never found one of their ancestors, they would forever wonder. I didn't want them to go a day without thinking that it could all end in an instant."

"I think it worked," said George. "These guys were desperate."

"Nicholas, in 2116, they developed the technology that enabled the Portal Finders to track people," said Hanna. "They couldn't track specific people, but they could follow tracks. Every time you go through a portal, some residue sticks to you. The new Portal Finders could track that. In 2136, they perfected it greatly, and they were much more efficient. But 2116 was the beginning. That's how George found you."

"And there are more of them out there," said Nicholas.

"But, why did you say *maybe* my Portal Finder will take me back home?" asked George. "They told me to follow the portals, and they will bring me back."

"They told you that to convince you to do the job," said Hanna. "You're never going home—none of you are. Portals aren't that simple. It's hard to find the right ones. Besides, I've been traveling for years and have never seen a portal that leads back to the 22nd century. They might exist, but I've never heard of them. They knew you'd never make it back."

George gave a stricken look.

"I knew that it sounded too easy. Bastards!"

"How were they supposed to know if we've killed Gates?"

"I have directions in my backpack to a spot to leave proof that you're dead. They said it will last all those years."

"And if they don't get the proof, they will assume that Nicholas is still alive," said Keith.

"Which means that they will do what I hoped," said Nicholas with a satisfied expression, "spend the rest of their lives with the fear of disappearing."

George looked at Hanna in fear.

"What now?"

"Now it ends," said Nicholas.

He picked up George's weapon, set it for kill, and calmly

pressed the button.

The weapon made the familiar popping sound, and a hole appeared in George's shirt. George slumped back as blood began to stain the front of his shirt.

"Oh," said Alice, putting her hands over her mouth.

"Did you have to kill him?" asked Randy.

"He did," said Hanna. "It was the only option."

Nicholas set the weapon on the bed and opened George's backpack.

"Shit!" he said under his breath.

"What?" asked Keith.

Nicholas pulled out George's Portal Finder. It had a hole through the center.

"He turned as I shot him," said Nicholas, "so my bullet went into his backpack and right through the Portal Finder. I was going to use it to go on my own. It's dangerous for you to be near me. It's better that I leave you."

He held up the destroyed Portal Finder.

"But now I can't."

Chapter 40

"You were leaving us?" asked Alice.

"You saw it yourself," said Nicholas. "My presence puts you all in danger. Besides, I'm a loner. I function better without having to worry about others."

"He's right about putting us all in danger," said Alex. "Unfortunately, we can't part with our Portal Finder."

There was no need to inform the others that their Portal Finder was a special one that could shut down all the other Portal Finders. It couldn't leave their hands. Alex saw that Hanna had her weapon out in case Nicholas decided he was desperate enough to kill for a Portal Finder.

That fear was alleviated by Alice.

"Keith, do we need ours? We're going with the others, and they have one. Could we give ours to Nicholas?"

Keith looked to Hanna for guidance.

"It makes sense to me," she said. "The portals might be in flux, but as long as we go through together, we'll at least land in the same place."

"Then, Nicholas, you can have ours," said Alice. "After all, it's partly yours anyway. We were all part of the same group."

"Thank you," said Nicholas. "I appreciate it. And no, Hanna, you never had to worry about me doing something violent to get it. I saw you getting your weapon ready. Even without a Portal Finder, I was probably going to leave."

Hanna relaxed her hand on the weapon.

"I do have a request, though," added Nicholas. "I need George's weapon. I have to put myself on an even playing field with the people coming after me."

There were no objections, so Nicholas thanked them and added the weapon to his backpack.

"I have a request of my own," said Hanna. "If you encounter other would-be assassins, please destroy their Portal Finders and weapons. We can't have them floating around out there. There are already too many of them unaccounted for."

"Including the one the man I shot in 1917 had," said Nicholas.

"That's why you hesitated," said Keith.

"It is. I wanted his Portal Finder and weapon, but the police were too close."

"Nothing can be done about that," said Hanna. "I understand. But please destroy any others you find—after exchanging a new one for your old one."

"You have my promise," said Nicholas. "Now, let's take care of George."

Getting the dead assassin out of the hotel was the priority. There was nothing to connect him to the group except a little blood on the wood floor and the bedspread. If the passersby who saw them together recognized him as the drunk man, it would be long after the group had left Fremont.

Using Randy and Alice as lookouts, Keith, Alex, and Nicholas carried the body out the back door and set him down behind a dumpster. Hanna threw the bedspread in the dumpster.

Back in the room, they cleaned the blood from the floor, leaving just a faint stain, and then they sat down to strategize.

"We should leave tonight," said Hanna. "We need a car."

"I suggest stealing one from a car dealer's lot," said Alex.

"Can you drive it?" asked Nicholas.

"Hey, I grew up in the 1950s. It'll be fun to drive one of these cars again."

"You're heading east," said Nicholas. "Can you drop me off in Omaha? From there, I can become invisible and figure out where to go. Staying here wouldn't be a good idea. The town is too small, and strangers always become the first suspects."

They quickly packed, then left through the back door.

"We're too conspicuous," said Nicholas. "Why don't the rest of you go down the street to the train station and wait for us? Alex and I will find the right car to steal. We may be a while."

Alex gave Hanna a quick kiss, and they were on their way.

Alex and Nicholas walked in silence for a few minutes, then Alex asked where Nicholas planned to go.

"I have no idea. I can't—and don't want to—go home. There's nothing for me there. Besides, I like the earlier times. My world was so crowded and dirty. This is clean. As I said, I'm a loner. Except for being a wanted man and the target of assassins from the future, I think I'm going to enjoy this."

On the edge of town, they ran across a Studebaker dealer.

"Perfect!" said Alex. "My first car was a Studebaker. Driving it will be easy for me."

The dealership had closed for the night, so the two men snuck onto the lot and checked out the cars.

"A 1950 Starlight Coupe," said Alex, stopping beside a robin's egg blue car. "This will do it. It might be a little tight until we reach Omaha, but once we kick you out, it'll be fine."

Nicholas chuckled.

"The keys will be inside on a hook," said Alex. "There won't be an alarm, so all we have to do is break in and grab them."

They went around to the service entrance, figuring the break-in would be less noticeable. Nicholas kicked open the door.

"You're stronger than you look," said Alex.

"I am, but for a door like this, it's all about the location of your kick."

Nicholas returned to the lot while Alex searched for the key. It took him a couple of minutes, but he eventually located it, as well as a license plate. As he left the building and approached the corner to the front lot, he saw Nicholas waving to him to get down. Alex ducked behind a car.

A night watchman had come onto the car lot, and Nicholas was observing him. If he went inside the building, he would discover the break-in. And they couldn't drive the car off the lot without him seeing them. So, Nicholas did the only logical thing. He set his weapon to stun and shot the man. The night watchman dropped to the ground. With Alex's help, he dragged the man to one of the cars and put him in the back seat.

"He should sleep for an hour or so," he said.

Alex attached the license plate to the car he had chosen, ripped off the tag in the window, and started the car, remembering the familiar purr of the engine. Nicholas climbed into the passenger seat, and Alex took off out of the car lot.

"This brings back a lot of memories," said Alex.

They drove through town, breathing sighs of relief when they passed a police car and it didn't start following them. When they reached the train station, the others piled in.

"A little crowded," said Hanna.

"It'll be better after Omaha," said Alex, "but this was the best car available."

They drove out of town without incident, intending to get as far from Fremont and the unconscious guard as quickly as possible.

They reached Omaha two hours later and parked in front of the train station. They all got out to say goodbye to Nicholas.

"Do you have enough money?" asked Keith.

"You have to ask me that?"

"Never mind," said Keith, laughing.

"Replenishing my money supply won't be a problem."

Alice hugged him.

"I feel like you are family," she said. "Thank you for all your help. I won't forget you."

Nicholas seemed awkward at the display of affection but was touched by it.

Keith also hugged him and said, "Watch your back."

"I will. And thank you both for the Portal Finder."

"Remember that it might not be accurate," said Hanna.

"It doesn't really matter. Where I end up is where I end up."

With some final goodbyes, the others climbed back into the car and drove off.

Nicholas stared after the car for a minute, then lifted his backpack and headed into the train station.

Chapter 41

Even with Nicholas gone, it was still a tight fit, but nobody minded. They were on their way to the next portal, and that was all that mattered. As strange as Nicholas had been, Keith and Alice missed him.

But they had other things to consider—mostly the love/hate anticipation of going home. They couldn't talk about it with Alex, Hanna, and Randy in the car, but they brought it up during a rest stop in Illinois. They had parked beside a large park, and they took a walk. It was the middle of the night, but they needed the air. The night was clear, with a million stars above them.

"It's beautiful," said Alice, holding onto Keith's arm.

"It is."

They sat on the grass, and Alice rested her head on Keith's shoulder.

"We could stay here, you know," said Alice.

"Don't think I haven't considered it," said Keith. "But don't you think it might get boring for us? Everything is old-fashioned. Can we live with that?"

"I'd like to think we could, but then I think about the stories Hanna and Alex told us in the car about their travels. Ray Burton and Natalie O'Brien thought they'd love that small town in England in 1959. They liked it for a while, then got bored. Hanna said it was the same for them when they were in 1902. Things were too slow for them. I guess we have to go to 2030."

"Alice, I'm not going to leave you for Cyndi. I've thought about it a lot. She and I were very happy together. I loved her. I still do, but everything is different now. She'll have been on her own for four years by the time we return, and maybe she will have found someone else. Either way, everything has changed. You are my life now."

They spent another half hour looking at the stars before Alex called them back to the car. They crowded back in, and Keith said, "You couldn't have stolen something bigger?"

While Keith and Alice were resting in the park, Alex had stolen the license plate off an Illinois car. Once the sun was up, he didn't know who would be coming after them. Better to have a different plate on the car, just in case.

As it turned out, they weren't stopped on their trip. Two days later, they drove across the Bourne Bridge, connecting Cape Cod to the mainland.

"Wow, I remember this," said Alex. "It's been many years, but it's all familiar."

"I was here in the 2020s," said Alice. "The bridge looks newer now, but the rest isn't all that different."

They drove in silence until they reached the village of Woods Hole, surrounded on three sides by water. They passed the terminal for the ferry to Martha's Vineyard and Nantucket, and turned up a side road.

"Our house is up here," said Alex.

"Alex, are you okay?" asked Hanna, who noticed he was shaking.

"I don't know. It's so strange. I'm on the way to my house—my house in 1950. I can't even begin to explain how weird this is. It was a lifetime ago, and yet, it feels like yesterday. I don't know whether to laugh or cry. I hated my trips to Cape Cod with my stuffy, overbearing parents, and yet, it holds a certain place in my heart."

None of the houses they passed looked lived in. Randy pointed it out.

"This area is the rich section," explained Alex. "These are all summer homes. The year-round residents live farther in from the water."

They pulled into the driveway of a large house overlooking Buzzard's Bay.

"Is this it?" asked Hanna.

"This is it."

"It's beautiful."

"Depends on your idea of beautiful," said Alex. "The view is beautiful. The memories, not so much."

The three-story house had an attached barn that doubled as a garage. Alex stopped the car in front of the garage.

"Let me get the key."

He went over to some bushes near the front door and picked up a rock. Underneath were keys to the house and garage. He opened the garage doors, which swung out to the sides. He got back in the car and pulled it inside. Then he got out and closed the doors behind him.

"We only used the garage during storms," he said, "but we always left it clean, in case we had to drive the car in quickly. I don't think we'll be bothered, but if we are, I'll just say I'm my father's brother."

"Hopefully, we won't be here long enough to get bothered," said Hanna.

It was getting dark, so they decided to check out the portal in the morning. In anticipation, they had stopped by a store and picked up a few things to eat and drink that night.

The curtains had all been closed for the winter, so Alex flicked a light switch. The light went on.

"Whew," he said. "I thought my parents left the electricity on in the winter, but I wasn't sure. The curtains are the heavy winter curtains, so I doubt anyone will see the light."

They spent some time touring the house and claiming bedrooms. With five bedrooms, there was plenty of room for everyone. Alex showed them his old room. The others felt that it was somewhat spartan, but Alex explained that it was how his parents wanted it.

"Warm and fuzzy, they were not," said Alex. He looked under the bed. "Hey, it's here."

He pulled out a cardboard shoebox and took off the lid.

"My Joe DiMaggio signed baseball! I thought someone had stolen it."

Then he looked at the others, his eyes wide.

"Oh my God! Someone *did* steal it. Me."

"What are you talking about?" asked Keith.

"I think I know," said Hanna, "and if I'm right, it's going to scramble your brain."

"Yeah, you're right," said Alex. "Okay, so here it is. The year didn't hit me until right now. In the summer of 1950, we arrived to find that we'd been robbed sometime over the winter. One of the things taken was my signed baseball. I couldn't understand how the thief knew that my baseball was in a shoebox under my bed."

"Whoa," said Randy. "Are you saying that it was you who stole from you? I thought you couldn't change history."

"We're not," said Hanna. "They were robbed in 1950. Who's to say that it wasn't us? I was told that some of my time-traveling friends experienced this before. The mystery writer, Beryl Dixon, disappeared in 1932, or thereabouts, and it's always been an unsolved mystery. My fellow time traveler, Herb Wells, met her that year, and they fell in love. A few months later, she went through the Hollow Rock portal to 1870. The big question was, did Herb change history by falling in love with her, or was that the very reason she mysteriously disappeared? Don't think about it too intensely, or you'll drive yourself crazy."

"Here's the thing," continued Alex. "Money was stolen from my father's safe--$15,000, to be exact. He never figured out how someone got the combination to the safe."

"What was he doing keeping that much cash in an empty house?" asked Alice.

"My parents lived through the Great Depression. They saw how quickly fortunes were lost. So, my father stashed cash all over the place—here, our house in Europe, and the basement of our house in New York. After the robbery, he took the money from here and never kept it here again. Something he never understood was that he had a lot more than $15,000 in the safe, but the robbers only stole that amount. This is how we get our seed money for our new lives in 2030—$5,000 for Hanna and me, $5,000 for Keith and Alice, and $5,000 for Randy."

"I feel bad stealing from your parents," said Alice.

"Don't. They were rich beyond belief and never donated to charities or causes. They were horrible people. This robbery was an annoyance to them. They didn't even miss it. I was more upset about my baseball than they were about the money."

Alex led them downstairs to his father's office. The safe was hidden behind a painting.

"Well, that's original," said Keith.

"They weren't very creative people," answered Alex.

He opened the safe to the sounds of drawn breath.

"Wow!" said Randy.

"Yeah, I think he always kept about $50,000 in here. That's why he couldn't understand someone only taking part of it."

He counted out $15,000 and divided it between the others.

"I really appreciate this," said Randy.

"Well, you kind of went through a tough time for the last thirty years. This won't make up for it, but it'll help. Just please don't tell anyone where you got it."

They sat down to eat, but no one was particularly hungry, so they went to bed early. They spent the night with a nervous anticipation of the next day. They'd be accessing a portal to 2030—or would they? That created some of the anxiety. The rest was generated by the fact that they would be going through a portal. For everyone except Alex and Hanna, it was still a new experience. But even Alex and Hanna were nervous.

"Why are we all so nervous?" asked Hanna, as they lay in bed.

"Because Randy will get to see his brother, we'll meet up again with Simone and the others, and Keith and Alice will start a new life in a familiar time. That's assuming the portal doesn't send us to some strange time. I'm also worried about you and Portal Sickness."

"Alex, I feel fine. Don't worry."

Hanna said it with all the confidence she could muster, but the fact was, although she wasn't showing any outward symptoms, she didn't feel fine. Her chest felt heavy, and her breathing was a bit labored. Luckily, Alex hadn't noticed it yet. She hoped it was due to nervousness or the long drive they had just completed. She had to get through the next portal. She just had to. Deep down, she knew it would be her last portal—it had to be a good one.

The next morning, after a sleepless night by all, they got in the car and drove to a stretch of high rocks lining the water.

"It's over there," said Hanna, looking at the Portal Finder. She pointed to the rocks.

They parked on the side of the road and crossed over to the rocks.

"Down at the bottom," said Hanna.

They gingerly crawled down the rocks to a flat area. Hanna looked at the Portal Finder, looked down, then looked back at the

Portal Finder.

"Oh no!" she said. "It's underwater!"

Chapter 42

"How far down?" asked Alex. "It's not very deep here."

"I'm checking." She adjusted the Portal Finder. "Not far below the surface—maybe five feet. There it is," she said, pointing, "In between those two rocks."

"It looks small," said Keith. "I don't think it will fit us all."

"I'm going down to check it out," said Alex. He pulled a small flashlight from his backpack.

"Take the Portal Finder so you don't accidentally go in," said Hanna.

"I will. I went in once without you. That's not going to happen again."

He and Hanna had slipped when accessing a portal that led back to the 1860s and ended up going through separately. They arrived several months apart, almost leading to disastrous results. They were determined never to let that happen again.

"It would be nice if I had a wetsuit," said Alex.

"I bet the water is cold," said Randy.

"I can guarantee it," said Alex. "It can be cold in the summer. This time of year, it's freezing. Before I go down to check it, we're all agreed, right? We're going to do this now?"

"Yes," said Randy.

"Of course," replied Hanna.

Keith and Alice nodded their heads, their nervousness apparent.

"You've done it before," Hanna said to them. "Don't worry."

"Okay," Alice said quietly.

"Okay then," said Alex. "Here I go."

He dropped into the water with a gasp. The temperature took his breath away. He let himself acclimate for a few seconds but couldn't bear it anymore. He had to get on with it. He slipped below the surface and, using the screen of the Portal Finder for reference, sank close to the portal. From five feet away, he shone the flashlight into the space between the rocks, then rose to the surface.

Randy and Keith helped him out of the water.

"Shit! That's cold," he said with chattering teeth.

He was shivering, so Hanna put his coat around his shoulders.

"It's small," he said, "too small for all of us. At most, two of us can go in at a time. Even that is going to be a tight squeeze."

"It sounds like I'll be going alone," said Randy. "I'm okay with that."

"Yes," Hanna said, "We'll have to break up. If the Portal Finder is correct, we'll all end up in 2030, but at different times. If it's not correct, I don't know what to tell you. Keith and Alice, maybe you shouldn't have given Nicholas your Portal Finder. But it's a little late for that, I guess."

"We're okay with whatever happens," said Alice.

"If we land in 2030, we're on our own," said Hanna. "If we land at a different time, we should check back here regularly to see if the others made it. How about the first of every month for a year? Try to be here by noon. If no one else shows up, it means we went to different times."

They all agreed.

"Then let's do this. Randy, you should go first, then Keith and

Alice. Don't forget to hold each other tight. Alex and I will bring up the rear in case someone has problems. Good luck to you all."

"Good thing I thought to put my baseball in a waterproof bag," said Alex.

They gave hugs all around, and then Randy slid down the rock into the water. After cursing about the water temperature a few times, he took a deep breath and swam down to the crack. One second, they could see him, and the next, he was gone.

Keith and Alice were next. Once in the water, they grabbed each other's wrists for a secure bond, then descended to the portal, where they disappeared.

"It's you and me," said Alex, getting back into the water.

Hanna joined him, gasping from the cold. They held on tight and swam for the crack between the rocks.

They nodded to each other in the murky water and entered the portal.

Chapter 43

RANDY

Randy was in the portal. What now? Did he go through? Well, he'd soon find out. He was running out of air. If he made it to the surface and the others were still there, he'd know that he'd done something wrong or that the portal didn't work.

He surfaced in the cold water and looked around. No one. It was sunny, unlike the cloudy day a few minutes earlier. And it was warm. The water was a lot warmer, too. Summer! That was perfect. When he was underwater, he had a momentary fear that he would surface, and it would be the middle of winter. He didn't have a coat, and his shoes would be ruined from the water.

Randy climbed out of the water and lay on one of the flat rocks. This was perfect! The sun would dry him and his clothes. He took off his shoes and set them next to him. He had been to Woods Hole twice before—both times during the summer. He remembered it as a casual place. Nothing extreme like Provincetown, but a place where no one would think twice if he walked through town barefoot.

He emptied his backpack and laid things out to dry. The night before, they all wrapped anything that they didn't want to get wet in plastic. Randy only had a few papers, like the response from his brother and the $5000.

Randy closed his eyes. Had he surfaced in 2030? He'd find out when he walked into town. Obviously, he wouldn't ask anyone what year it was, but he could check for calendars. If he bought anything, he could check the receipt—at least, he assumed that receipts in 2030 would still be the same as they were in 2009.

He must have fallen asleep, because the next time he opened his eyes the sun was in a different place, and his clothes were mostly dry. He panicked and checked for his money. It was still there.

What now?

Easy. He would catch a bus and head to Florida to see his brother. At least, he assumed his brother was still there. He was in 2026.

Randy felt so grateful to Alex and Hanna. He had told them that before they all went into the portal. They didn't need to save him in Tucson, but they did. And now, thanks to Alex, he had money to get around. First, he needed to buy clothes and find a place to stay for the night. Tomorrow, he would catch the bus.

Randy began to shiver, and it wasn't from the temperature. He was from 2009, but he really wasn't. He had spent the last thirty years in the late 1800s. He had probably forgotten a lot of what he knew in 2009. Was he even going to be able to survive? If he could make it to his brother, he would be fine.

Maybe he could call Natalie for help. No, that would be silly. He was told that Natalie was back to acting. Did he really think she would take a call from him?

No, he had to get to his brother. Or even better, have his brother come to him. He just needed to use a phone. His brother put his phone number at the bottom of his note, just in case.

Randy quickly shoved his belongings into his backpack. His shoes were still wet, but he put them on anyway. It wasn't more than a mile to the town of Woods Hole, and it was warm, so it made for an easy walk.

As he walked, he thought about the others. Did they make it okay? That portal was tiny. He had just barely fit himself. Two people would be a tight fit, especially if carrying backpacks. And what would happen if one person went through and was still holding onto the other person who couldn't fit? Would just one of them go? Luckily, he didn't have to worry about it, but he was concerned for his friends. Assuming they made it, did they arrive before or after him? They had no plans to meet if they made it to 2030, so unless he ran into them by accident, he had probably seen the last of any of them.

He reached the town.

Something wasn't right. What was it?

Tourists. There were very few tourists. Why would that be? He remembered Woods Hole as a booming place in the summer, with tourists everywhere. Was he wrong about the time of year? Maybe it was just a warm spring day, and the tourist season hadn't started yet.

No, there was something else.

Businesses were closed. Not all of them, but some smaller ones had CLOSED signs, and the windows were empty of product. Had the world just suffered a Depression? After all, the most recent message he had from his brother was from 2026. Plus, Keith and Alice were from 2026. They didn't indicate any problems. Anything could have happened after that.

He would have to ask some questions, but he'd have to be careful how he asked them.

The first business he encountered was a drugstore. He walked in and was immediately struck by the half-empty shelves. He saw a picture of a sailboat on a magazine cover and knew exactly how he'd approach it.

"This may sound like a strange question," he asked a man behind the pharmacy counter, "but what happened?"

A calendar behind the pharmacist showed that it was August 2030. He had made it!

"What do you mean?" the man asked. He was about Randy's age, with a tired look about him.

"I've been living on my sailboat for the last year—off the grid, so to speak—and I've returned to everything looking different."

He hoped that being away for a year was enough time, and that whatever it was hadn't happened earlier than that.

"Are you kidding me?" asked the man. "You had no access to the Internet or GPS? How did you navigate?"

"By hand, the old-fashioned way. It seemed like a good idea at the time, but I missed civilization and the modern conveniences."

Randy hoped he was convincing, but what else could he say? *I'm a time traveler who just arrived here?*

It seemed to work. Although amazed by it, the pharmacist seemed to accept it.

"Well then, you have a lot to catch up on. In a sense, we've all been living off the grid for the last eight months. The cloud collapsed."

Luckily, Randy was somewhat familiar with the concept from 2009, and a few conversations with Keith and Alice about what to expect in 2030 had helped. Of course, their knowledge ended in 2026, but the concepts still applied.

"What do you mean the cloud collapsed? The whole thing or parts of it?"

"Hell if I know. It's all the same to me. All I know is that it affected everything—phones, Internet, the supply chain ... you name it. That's why you see so many empty stores. They all went out of business. It's worse than the pandemic."

Keith and Alice had also filled him in on the pandemic. What would he have done without their knowledge?

The man continued. "It's taken eight long months, but things are starting to come back. Smartphones are still having trouble, and the Internet is spotty, but the supply chain is slowly getting fixed, as is the banking. But let me tell you, people lost a lot. People went bankrupt overnight. And personal data—pictures and documents stored on the cloud … POOF! Gone. The government says they were prepared for it, but they weren't. We're just lucky it wasn't worse than it was with protests and riots. Somehow, it didn't turn into total anarchy. And you knew nothing of this?"

"As unbelievable as it sounds, no, I didn't. You mentioned phones. I haven't spoken to my brother in Florida in over a year and was going to call him. Are you saying that I might not get through?"

"If he has a smartphone, probably not. Remember the old flip phones?"

"I sure do."

In fact, that's what he had when he went through the portal at Hollow Rock. But he had long since lost it.

"Well, that's what we're going back to while they repair the cloud. They work just fine. Let me guess, you don't have a phone."

Randy shook his head. "One of the things I got rid of."

"Still got his number? I can try it for you."

"Would you? I'd really appreciate it."

He gave the man Sammy's number, and the pharmacist dialed. He listened for a minute, then said, "Nope. Your brother must still have a dead smartphone. I'm getting the 'out of service' tone. You should go visit him."

"I would sail down, but my boat sustained a fair amount of damage in the last storm I encountered. Are the buses running?"

"They are now. For a while, nothing was running. All their schedules and payment methods were online. They all disappeared. But the transportation industry was one of the first to get going again. There'll be a bus coming through here in about an hour. It'll take you to Boston. From there, you can find one to Florida. Bus stops right here. I can sell you a ticket."

Change of plans, thought Randy. *I can sleep on the bus.*

"Thanks for all your help. Yes, I'll take a ticket to Boston. And I'll get some snacks from you and some toiletries. Is there any place I can pick up some new clothes?"

The man directed him to a store down the street. After Randy had filled his backpack with his purchases, he went to the clothing store and picked up a couple of outfits, including socks and sneakers.

When the bus arrived, Randy felt like a new man. He waved to the pharmacist and got on the bus, hoping his brother was still in the same place.

*****

Two days later, the bus pulled into Fort Lauderdale. Randy caught a cab from the bus station to his brother's house. An old Jeep sat out front.

It's something Sammy would own, he thought.

He crossed his fingers and rang the bell.

The door opened, and there he was! Sammy was twenty-one years older than when he last saw him, but then, Randy was thirty years older.

"Yes?" said Sammy, squinting from the brightness of the sun behind Randy.

Going through the portal at Hollow Rock, almost dying in the middle of the desert, all his years stuck in the 1800s, and all the time missing his family, suddenly melted away. Randy had made it back.

"Hi, Sammy," he said with tears running down his cheeks.

"It's me."

Chapter 44

KEITH AND ALICE

They had to get out of the portal!

Alice squeezed out the opening, still holding Keith's hand. He came out immediately after her. They only let go when they reached the surface. It was night, but the air was warm. The water was chilly but not freezing.

They climbed up onto the rocks.

"Did we make it?" asked Alice.

"I don't know," said Keith. "None of the others are here."

"Hanna said that would probably happen, though. We could land months apart."

"Let's find a car," said Keith. "We can check the license plate for the date. We'll see what year it says. I see one down the block."

Now, they were cold. The night air had chilled them. Keith knew they'd have to find a place to warm up and get dry clothes.

As they approached the car, Keith got a bad feeling. The car had the boxiness of cars from the 1970s and 80s.

"It doesn't look like a modern car," said Alice.

"I was just thinking that."

Keith knelt behind the car and peered at the license plate. A cloud moved from in front of the moon, making things brighter. The tag read: DEC '74.

1974!

Keith sat on the ground. He breathed slowly, trying not to panic.

"We didn't make it to 2030," he said.

"What year?" asked Alice.

"The tag says 1974. That tag is good through December, so I'm guessing it's autumn. And unless Alex and Hanna came to this same time, this is where we'll have to stay, because we gave Nicholas the Portal Finder."

Keith was doing his best to keep from throwing up.

"Hey! What are you people doing near my car?"

A man was standing on the porch of his house.

"Sorry," said Keith. "I tripped. I'm okay now, and we'll be on our way."

"You're sure you're okay?"

"I am, thank you—just a scraped knee. We've lost track of time. Can you tell me the date?"

"The date? September 14th."

"Thank you."

"September 14th, 1974," Keith said as they walked away.

"Keith, are you okay? You're breathing strangely."

Keith walked over to the rocks at the edge of the water.

"I was starting to have a panic attack. I think I'm better now … maybe. Alice, we're stuck in 1974. We don't have a Portal Finder, and we don't have Alex and Hanna to turn to for advice."

"Maybe they came here, too," said Alice.

"My gut tells me they didn't, but you could be right. But what if they didn't? This is it. This is where we are. It's a foreign time for us both."

"But we're together. We'll make it through any obstacles we run up against."

"You're right," said Keith. "I'm sorry. It was a momentary bit of panic."

"We're both going to have them," said Alice. "I'm never

going to see my parents again. I've cried many times over that, and that's okay. We can't expect to go through time with constant smiles on our faces. Today, it's your panic attack. Tomorrow, it'll be mine. And sometimes we might both have them at the same time. But we'll make it through."

They sat on the rock, holding each other. Finally, Keith stood up.

"I'll bet Alex's parents still own the house," he said. "Being September, they probably aren't there. Let's see if we can break in and get some dry clothes. But let's remember. We don't have a Portal Finder. We can't do anything blatantly illegal. We have nowhere to escape to."

"You mean we can't rob any banks?" asked Alice with a smile.

"If you do, don't tell me about it."

Keith was feeling back to normal. He didn't know how long it would last, though.

Fifteen minutes later, they reached Alex's house. It was pitch black, like all the other houses on the block.

"Perfect," said Keith.

"Did they have alarms back then—or rather, now?" asked Alice.

"Honestly? I have no idea."

They quickly discovered that this house didn't have an alarm system. Keith checked the spot where Alex found the key in 1950. He had to search a bit, but then found it.

"The key is in the same spot, so I'm sure it's their house," he said.

The first thing they did was to check to make sure the house was vacant, and that all the curtains were closed.

"We still shouldn't turn on any lights," said Alice.

"I agree, but we can use flashlights if we find any."

They checked all the kitchen drawers and found two

flashlights. They also found an envelope addressed to Alex's parents, so that confirmed they still owned the house. They climbed the stairs to the bedroom they had used in 1950. Other than being marginally updated, it hadn't changed much at all. They looked in Alex's old bedroom. It had been turned into a storage room.

"Kinda sad," said Keith.

"It is. The whole story of Alex's childhood was sad."

"I think we should stay here tonight, and decide what to do tomorrow," said Keith.

They rooted around in the kitchen for food and found some cans of beef stew, which they heated and ate in the dark.

*****

They were lying in bed in each other's arms when Alice whispered in Keith's ear.

"Keith?" She wasn't sure if he had fallen asleep.

He squeezed her to show he was awake.

"I keep thinking about what Nicholas said."

"Which thing?" Keith asked in a sleepy voice.

"That you were his target because the top Interpol agent was related to you."

"Yes, that was a bit disturbing." He sounded more awake now.

"I've thought about it a lot," said Alice. "When he first said it, I assumed it was a child of a child of a child, etc., that you were going to have with Cyndi, and that depressed me. It meant we were going back, and you'd be getting back together with Cyndi. I knew I should be happy for you, but I wasn't, and I felt very selfish thinking it. But now I realize that unless Cyndi was pregnant when you left—"

"She wasn't. We weren't ready for children."

"Okay, then if she wasn't, and there is no chance we are going back to that time—"

"Then it means he will be related to you and me."

"Yes."

"But I'm still not ready for kids."

"Oh god, I'm not either. The thought of having children with you makes me happy, but not now. However, that wasn't my point. It brought up two questions. First, why was he going after you and not both of us—or either one of us? He was clear that you were the target. After all, they would know who the mother is. Second, it disturbs me that a possible descendant of mine could be involved in something so horrible."

"To address the second point first," said Keith, "no one has control over the actions of their descendants, and if we start to worry about that, it's going to drive us crazy. All we can hope for is that it was all stopped before something catastrophic could happen. As for your first point, I don't know. Maybe Nicholas knew but knew he only had to kill one of us or was uncomfortable killing a woman. Maybe their records weren't as good as we would assume they were. I don't think we'll ever have the answer to that."

He pulled her closer.

"Our dilemma was taken care of. Wasn't it Hanna who told us not to worry because we never knew what the portals would do? Well, this one sent us to 1974. Maybe it's not the ideal time. We'll have to brush up on our history and unlearn a lot of what we have come to accept as normal. But the important thing is we're together. Just know that I'm devoted to you. We're going to have a great life together. I love you."

"I love you, too."

They lay quietly, just enjoying the silence. Then Alice asked, "Keith, do you ever think about Barbara and Pete?"

"Not much, I'm afraid," answered Keith. "Only because I

never really knew them that well. They were your friends."

"I've thought about them a lot lately. I don't think things went well for them. It's a gut feeling."

"You're probably right. Even if they lived through the war, they are now stuck in that era. I wouldn't wish that on anyone. I guess all we can hope for is that they did make it through, and that they found each other and are happy."

"But I don't think that's what happened," said Alice.

"No, I don't think so."

"How everything changed when Pete fell through that hole. It all happened in a second."

"But I found you because of it," said Keith.

"You did. And I couldn't be happier."

*****

They woke up refreshed the next morning, ready to move on.

"We have $5,000 to start our new life with," said Keith.

They were on their way to downtown Woods Hole to find transportation to Boston.

"I think $5,000 went a long way in the 1970s," Keith continued, "so I bet we can find an inexpensive apartment. We won't need a car, so we don't have to worry about getting a license immediately. I bet we can find jobs that pay under the table until we find a way to become official. There are always ways around that."

"And then what?"

"Then we save as much money as we can to invest."

"Invest in what?"

"Alice, what do we know that no one else knows?"

"The future."

"Exactly."

Chapter 45

ALEX AND HANNA

"What does the Portal Finder say?" asked Hanna.

"October 4th, 2015. We missed it by fifteen years," said Alex. "We're close though. Better than the 1700s."

"It is. I wonder, though. Was it the same for all of us? Did we all land here, or did it shift for each of us?"

"All we can do is what we agreed on and meet here every month for a year. In the meantime, I'm cold."

It was a sunny day, but an autumn chill was in the air.

"Are you two okay?"

A police car had pulled up beside them.

"Thank you, officer," said Alex. "We are. My wife slipped on the rocks. We were holding hands, so we both went in. We're wet, but okay."

"Can I drive you anywhere?"

"We took the bus from Boston to Woods Hole. We should have gotten off in Falmouth, but we hadn't seen Woods Hole, so we came here. Now, we need to get back to Falmouth."

"Hop in. I'll take you."

"We'll get your seat wet."

"Not a problem. Where can I take you?"

"Maybe just Main Street. Dry clothes are a priority."

The officer asked them a few innocent questions on the road to Falmouth, but nothing they couldn't answer. Two hours later, they were in an inexpensive hotel, wearing new clothes.

"What now?" asked Alex.

"I'm not sure. Landing here makes things more complicated. We can't make ourselves known to Ray and the others until after his last communication from us," said Hanna. "I know we can't change history—or at least, I don't think so—but I somehow feel that if we contact him before that date, we're going to screw up the time continuum. I don't know what the result would be, but we can't do it. We can't make ourselves known to Ray or any of the others until then. What was the date of the last communication?"

"August 26th, 2026, was the date he put on it."

"Then we have to shoot for some time after that."

"That's eleven years from now," said Alex. "Do we wait or look for another portal that can take us closer to that date? As much as I hate to wait, who knows if we'll ever find a portal to get us closer, especially now that we can't trust them for their accuracy? Besides, I don't think you're being honest about feeling okay. I don't think you are feeling okay at all."

"I've been a bit tired lately, but I don't think it's Portal Sickness."

Alex stared at her.

"Okay, maybe I've got a touch of it, but it's nothing serious."

"I wish you had told me before we went through this portal."

"And be stuck in 1950? Alex, I'm willing to take the chance."

"I'm not. I'd rather be with you in the 1700s than without you here. But, like I said before, you did this on purpose. If you die, at least I'll be near friends. The problem is that you assumed it would be 2030 and I'd have instant access to them. But it's not. It doesn't matter anyway. Don't you get it, Hanna? I love you and would be lost if you died."

"We're all going to die at some point," said Hanna unconvincingly.

"But it doesn't have to be now," said Alex. "However, what's done is done. We have other things to think about. We need to get jobs, and we need to find a place to live. We need Social Security cards to get jobs. I have one, but it shows that I was born in 1935. That makes me eighty. I don't look eighty, although I certainly feel it much of the time. Just as important—or maybe more important—I'm already overwhelmed, and we haven't even joined society. Hanna, I'm from 1973. Do you have any idea how much I need to learn? I don't, and that's the scary part. I have so much to catch up on and don't even know where to start."

"This is all new to me, too," said Hanna.

"Yes, but for you, it's a case of dumbing down. That's a lot easier to do."

Hanna saw that Alex was about to have a panic attack.

"Okay, stop! Alex, please take a breath."

He closed his eyes and breathed. When he seemed calmer, she continued.

"I get it, Alex. I get it more than you think I do. Until now, you've always been able to look at a time through the eyes of a history teacher. In 1950, it was through the eyes of someone who had experienced it. Now, you are in a completely different situation. Now, you are behind the curve and need to catch up."

"Way behind."

"Okay, way behind. But you're a smart person. You'll find a way to prioritize your learning. I can help you with some of it. Although history isn't my strong point, technology is. I can bring you up to date on anything technical. I can show you how to use a computer. Once you get comfortable with that, you can be your own teacher. Make a list of everything you want to know, then one by one, read up on them on the computer. There are places on the computer for you to ask any kind of question. It will locate the answer and present it to you. It might take you a few months, but you'll be up to date."

Alex had calmed down.

"Okay," he said, "I'll take your word for it. But we still have the two big problems in front of us—money and housing. And I'd rather not have to rob a bank to get the money. We have $5,000. That won't last us very long."

"I'm working on it."

They spent the next day in the library. Hanna figured out how to use the computer, and after some trial and error, felt comfortable with Google. She searched how to obtain a fake Social Security card and decided the easiest way was to find a forger. Once she was familiar with the archaic workings of their computer and the Internet, she incorporated her computer skills from the 22nd century. She searched online to find sites that most people didn't even know existed. From there, she found a forger in Boston who could make them Social Security cards and birth certificates. They had him make two sets of documents for each of them with different names and numbers in case something went wrong, and they needed to change their identities.

When they arrived at his shop off a dank alley to pick them up, the $1000 fee suddenly became $3000.

"You don't want to do that," said Hanna to the small, squirrelly man in the darkened office.

"You don't have much choice, honey. You and your man are desperate, and I fully intend to take advantage of that."

"Big mistake," said Alex.

"I don't think so," said the little man, pulling out a gun.

"Do you treat all your customers this way?" asked Hanna.

"No. I have my regulars. I only treat the desperate ones this way. You qualify in that category."

His head dropped on his desk as Alex hit him with a blast

from his weapon.

"I just stunned him," he said.

"That's good," said Hanna. "We're going to have to kill him, though. He'll send people looking for us. In the meantime, we make sure any trace of us is gone from here. He's also going to help us financially," she added, eyeing the safe against the wall.

Once upon a time, the thought of killing someone would have made Alex sick, but times had changed, and ridding the world of a scumbag like this guy seemed a necessary service.

They went through his records, found all the information the man had compiled on them, and put them through his shredder, keeping only the Social Security cards and birth certificates.

When the man woke up and saw Hanna and Alex standing over him, he knew he was in trouble.

"What did you hit me with?"

"Doesn't matter," said Hanna. "What matters is what we will hit you with if you don't open your safe."

"No way."

Hanna took the weapon from Alex, set it to "kill," and pointed it at the man's hand.

"I'm counting to three, and you lose a finger or two. One…"

"What the hell is that?"

"Two…"

"No way am—"

"Three."

A pop sounded, and his hand spurted blood as two fingers were blown away. The man screamed and held his hand close to his chest, using his shirt to stop the blood.

"You'll lose a foot next," said Hanna.

"Okay, okay. 5-24-35."

While Hanna covered him with the weapon, Alex went to the safe and dialed the combination. The safe opened, revealing stacks of bills.

"Goodness," said Alex. "Business must be good."

"You can't steal that," said the man. "I'll have so many people after you; you'll spend the rest of your life looking over your shoulder."

"Maybe," said Hanna, "but you won't."

A pop sounded, and a red splotch appeared on the man's shirt. He slumped over dead.

They found a carry-on bag and loaded it with the cash. Then they checked outside carefully before leaving, quickly making their way down the street. They eventually arrived at the bus station, where they took a bus back down to Cape Cod and their hotel room in Falmouth.

When they finished counting what they had stolen, it totaled over $75,000 in denominations of all sizes.

Most importantly, they now had Social Security cards and birth certificates, allowing them to get jobs and passports, and become legitimate members of society.

*****

Six months passed. With the original $5,000, they had bought a used computer. It took Hanna less than a week to know everything there was to know about it so she could start teaching Alex. Hanna used her scientific background and applied for a job in Boston at a biotech firm, having forged a resume. It took less than a week for people there to start listening to her ideas on where she thought the field was heading, and ways to take advantage of it. Alex and Hanna moved to Boston, where they found a place not too far from where fellow time traveler Uncle Jim Lawrence was living. However, Hanna knew better than to contact him.

They returned to the portal in Woods Hole at the appointed time every month but saw no sign of their friends. They were reaching the conclusion that they were the only ones who had landed in 2015.

Hanna's salary and the Boston windfall allowed Alex to stay home to learn all he could about 2015 and the years back to 1973. He began in 1973 and learned the historical, social, and cultural news for each year up to the current one. Once he was well-versed in the history, he brought himself up to date technologically. He was now to the point of deciding what he wanted to do for work.

All of that was temporary, though. Their passports had arrived, and they were saving as much money as possible. They also still had most of the money from the forger. When they felt they had reached a comfortable level in their savings, Hanna would take a leave of absence so they could travel the world.

And then Hanna got sick.

Chapter 46

Their worst nightmare had come true.

They thought they had dodged a bullet when the minor issues Hanna felt after accessing the final portal disappeared a week later.

Several months after Hanna took the job in Boston, the breathing issues began to creep back in. At first, they thought she had picked up a cold. Because it had been so long, Portal Sickness wasn't even considered. When the cold turned into a cough, they began to get concerned. Finally, Hanna went to a doctor.

"I know that doctors are supposed to have all the answers," the doctor said after giving her a thorough examination, "but I don't know what you have. You have the beginnings of pneumonia. We can treat that. But pneumonia is only one aspect of this. Pneumonia in conjunction with the rash concerns me."

"What rash?" asked Hanna.

"The rash on your back. You didn't know you had it?"

Alex looked at it and said, "That rash wasn't there this morning."

"You're sure?"

"Absolutely."

"And now it's appearing on your arms," said the doctor. "It wasn't there a minute ago. I'd say that the skin condition was a fast-moving allergic reaction, but when considered in conjunction with the pneumonia, we're dealing with something else. You'll have to excuse me for a moment."

The doctor quickly left the room.

"Did Fletch tell us the signs of Portal Sickness?" asked Alex.

"I don't think they knew all the signs," said Hanna. She broke into a coughing fit. When it was finished, she said, "He told us about the respiratory problems, but I don't think he knew anything beyond that. What do you think the doctor is doing?"

"I think he's calling for help. He has no idea what's going on. If I had to guess, they will isolate you—maybe both of us. So, the question is, do we leave now or let them do it?"

"Fletch and I were discussing Portal Sickness before we left," said Hanna. "He felt that something as simple as a common antibiotic could work on it. But they didn't have antibiotics until more recent times, and most of the Eliminators were traveling in earlier times."

"Penicillin was the first antibiotic," said Alex. "That came about in the 1940s. The 1950s started the antibiotic boom."

"How do you know that?"

"I was a history teacher, remember?"

"Maybe he will prescribe an antibiotic," said Hanna.

They waited close to an hour for the doctor to return. They had almost decided to leave when the doctor walked in the room dressed in a biohazard suit.

"That's not good," whispered Alex.

"There's an ambulance outside to take you to the hospital," said the doctor. "We don't know what you have, and since you work for a biotech firm, it's possible that you caught something there."

"I'm not around any of that stuff," said Hanna. "I work in an office doing research and computations. I don't touch anything dangerous."

"Nevertheless," said the doctor, "we can't take any chances."

"I'm sure all I need is an antibiotic," said Hanna.

"Please, let us figure out what you need," said the doctor. "I'm afraid both of you will have to come with us. Alex, we don't know if you've become infected. We have to put you both in quarantine."

"Could you at least try an antibiotic first?" asked Hanna.

"No, we don't want to try anything until we have something to go on. We can't risk giving you the wrong medicine. There are specialists at the hospital to deal with this. I'm afraid you don't have a choice. If you have something contagious, you could create an epidemic."

"It's not contagious," said Alex.

"You don't know that."

Alex looked at Hanna and threw up his hands.

"Okay, we'll go," said Hanna. "But we are keeping our backpacks with us. We have too many important things in there."

"I'm sure that won't be a problem," said the doctor.

Alex knew exactly why Hanna had said that. Their weapons were in the backpacks, and they never went anywhere without their backpacks. Besides not wanting the weapons discovered by the hospital staff, they knew they might need them to escape if conditions necessitated it.

They followed the doctor, who led them to two other men in hazmat suits, who brought them outside to a waiting ambulance. Along the way, they noticed that the doctors' offices had been cleared out. The staff were all outside, standing well back from the door. A police car with lights flashing sat next to the ambulance.

They were herded into the rear of the ambulance. A paramedic accompanied them and hooked Hanna up to various machines.

Alex was scared. Hanna looked worse than she had just minutes earlier. The rash had crept onto her neck. They didn't want to say anything in front of the paramedic, so Alex just held Hanna's hand.

The ambulance sped through the streets of Boston with the police car leading the way. They arrived at a hospital—Alex had no idea which one—a few minutes later. When they arrived, they were told to put on protective suits and were led into the building. They were taken through a back entrance down a series of corridors to a glassed-in area, where they were directed to a small exam room in the back.

They were told they could take off their protective suits by the paramedic.

"Hang in there," he said, putting his gloved hand on Hanna's shoulder. Then he left the room.

They were alone.

"How do you feel?" asked Alex.

"Sick."

Hanna was white as a sheet. She laid down on the exam table but immediately started coughing. Alex had tears in his eyes.

Hanna reached out and held Alex's hand.

"It'll be okay," she said.

Alex shook his head. "This is what I was afraid of. It has to be Portal Sickness. Why else would the doctors be so baffled by it?"

"One doctor was. It doesn't mean they all will be."

"Hey, the rash on your back is gone," said Alex. "Maybe that's why we didn't see a rash on any of the Eliminators who had it. Maybe it comes and goes."

The next few hours were spent with doctors poking and prodding Hanna, taking blood, and doing X-rays and MRIs. The rash had disappeared entirely, which confounded the doctors. One of the doctors finally started her on an antibiotic for the pneumonia. In general, the doctors and nurses were friendly and concerned.

Late in the day, they were moved to a room with two beds.

Nurses came in three more times that day and took blood from them.

"Do you think they found something?" asked Alex.

"I do," replied Hanna, slapping her forehead. "And I know what it is. I can't believe I was so stupid."

The antibiotic had kicked in, and she was already feeling much better. She still had the cough, but it had quieted down. As they had thought, it looked like the Portal Sickness could be cured by a simple antibiotic, something none of the Eliminators had access to.

"What do you mean?" asked Alex.

"They are going to find something, and they're not going to know what it is or how it got there, which means they will keep me here and run more tests on me. When those are inconclusive, they'll send me to a special lab. I can map it out right now. I can tell you exactly how this is going to go. Alex, we have to get out of here."

"What are you talking about?"

"Around the year 2100, doctors discovered that people's blood was breaking down. The air pollution worldwide was starting to kill people in ways that it never had before, and blood was the key. If they could figure out how to protect the bloodstream from the pollution, people would be healthier, and fewer deaths would result."

"Let me guess. They added something to your blood."

"They did. It was a chemical designed to keep the blood healthy. One shot was all you'd ever need, and the chemical would stay in your blood for life. It was an amazing, life-changing discovery. The developers won a Nobel prize for their work. All the time travelers were told never to go to the doctor unless absolutely necessary, especially in modern times like now, when they had the equipment to discover the anomaly in our blood. Alex, we really have to get out of here."

"I think they're going to let me go," said Alex. "When they do, I'll head home and gather everything we'll need, including the passports and credit cards under our alternate name. After I grab all that stuff, I'll come back and get you out of this place. Say goodbye to your job. It's time to go on the run and start seeing the world."

Chapter 47

As expected, they let Alex go later that day but told Hanna she'd have to stay longer.

"We're seeing some anomalies in your blood that concern us," explained the doctor. "Overall, your blood is healthy, but we've discovered something we can't explain—something that seems to have been added to your blood. It makes no sense to any of us. We might need to have you looked at by someone else."

Alex and Hanna knew that the "someone else" would be people who would treat Hanna like a lab rat at some secret location. They could tell that the doctors were becoming suspicious about what it could possibly be. They were probably now thinking along the lines of espionage, terrorism, or something that would lead to a world crisis.

"It was that unique," Hanna had told Alex. "It's going to raise all kinds of suspicions."

So now, Alex was on a mission, and he couldn't waste any time. Who knew when they'd move her? If they were beginning to think that her blood contained something suspicious, they might not even tell Alex. They might also put Hanna under intense scrutiny and discover that she wasn't the Mildred Mayer that her license indicated.

Yes, he had to move fast.

He caught a cab back to the doctor's office where they had left their car, then drove to their apartment in East Boston. As he exited the car, he saw a car parked a block away that didn't fit in with the rest of the working-class neighborhood.

He was already being watched.

Well, he could deal with that later. His goal was to get everything they'd need to disappear. He went to the closet and pulled out the two suitcases that contained their "flight" clothes—the clothes they'd need if they had to leave quickly. He pulled out all the cash from their safe—over $60,000. It was money left over from robbing the forger, along with extra money from Hanna's paychecks. His backpack already contained his weapon. Now he added their Portal Finder. They had no intention of ever using it again, but it was important to always keep it close to them.

From one of the suitcases, Alex pulled out his disguise kit. He pasted on a mustache, a close-cropped beard, and a wig that turned his short brown hair into black hair, streaked with gray, that covered the tops of his ears.

He changed into a new outfit and looked at himself in the mirror. Brown-haired, clean-cut Logan Mayer, his previous persona—and husband of Hanna's Mildred Mayer—had become black-haired Alex Snow, with a beard and mustache.

They had decided that if they had to switch to their new names, they'd be close to the names they had always known each other as. So, Alex Frost became Alex Snow. Hanna Landers became Hanna Snow, whose maiden name (in case anyone asked) was Flanders.

Alex was ready. First things first. He left everything piled in the living room and went down the stairs to the front door. With his weapon in his pocket, he crossed the road and walked down the block toward the suspicious car. As he approached, he saw a man and a woman in the front seats. He reached the car and rapped on the driver's window. The driver rolled it down.

"What?"

"You wouldn't happen to be watching Logan Mayer, would you?"

"Move along."

"I just wanted to tell you that he slipped out the back using the fire escape."

Now he had their attention. They looked at each other, and the woman reached for a radio. Alex calmly stunned her with his weapon, then turned it on the driver and repeated it. Alex looked at his watch. They would be unconscious for about an hour, so he didn't have much time. The woman had a camera in her lap. They had been taking pictures of him! Alex was beginning to realize just how serious the situation was. He grabbed the camera and walked calmly back to his apartment. With a quick look around the apartment, he took everything he'd packed, loaded his car, and drove off.

They wouldn't miss the apartment. Somehow, they knew it would all be temporary, although this wasn't how Alex saw them leaving.

As he got out of his car in the hospital parking garage, his phone buzzed. It was a text from Hanna.

Where are you? They are taking me somewhere. Going by ambulance, I think. Leaving the room in a minute. Please be close.

He quickly texted back: *I'm here. Will go to where they brought us in.*

Alex grabbed his weapon and locked the car. He ran down the stairs to the street level and across to the hospital. He was pretty sure he could find where they had come before—they had driven around to the back of the hospital.

Could he make it in time?

The hospital was enormous. Finding the rear of the building was difficult, as he kept running into dead ends. Finally, he found a back driveway that seemed familiar. He turned a corner, and there it was—an ambulance with the engine running.

He needed to do this correctly, with no one seeing his face. His new look was only as good as his anonymity.

Before proceeding, he looked around carefully. There it was—a camera near the back entrance to the hospital. It was stationary, pointing down to the spot where the ambulance waited. How much peripheral vision did the camera have?

He heard a sound behind him. A garbage truck had pulled into the alleyway and was heading his way. Just beyond the ambulance was a dumpster. Perfect!

As the garbage truck passed him, Alex walked behind it. The driver couldn't see him, so he'd never be able to identify Alex. As the truck passed the ambulance, the rear door was open. Alex stepped out from behind the garbage truck and stepped behind the open door to the ambulance. Again, the driver couldn't see him.

An EMT or paramedic was preparing for Hanna's arrival. Before he could turn around, Alex stunned him. The man dropped to the floor. Alex made sure he was in a comfortable position and wasn't hurt.

Alex waited by the rear of the ambulance. He had to time this just right—destroying the camera close enough to Hanna's exit so it wouldn't bring security before Hanna arrived.

Coming out.

Perfect. Thank you, Hanna!

Alex set the weapon to "kill" and aimed at the camera over the door, keeping himself hidden. He pushed the button, and the camera blew into a hundred pieces. Alex moved over to the front of the ambulance, hiding behind the fender.

The door opened, and six people walked out, including Hanna. Alex had reset the weapon to "stun," As soon as they passed him, he carefully took five quick shots. The people accompanying Hanna dropped to the ground.

"Hi, Honey, I'm here."

"Thank you, handsome." She looked up. "And you remembered the camera on the wall. You've become quite sneaky."

"I had a good, sneaky teacher. We need to go. The car is in the parking garage. They had a couple watching me at the house, but I took care of them. They are the only ones who saw my disguise, but I don't think they'll connect it to me. They'll eventually look up our car in the system and be on the lookout for it, but we probably have a little time. Airport?"

"Yes, but not Boston," said Hanna. "One of the airports around New York would be better. Things will get too hot around here."

"We can leave now," said Alex. "I have everything in the car ready to go."

When they reached the car, Hanna took out her disguise kit before they left the garage.

"I'll put it on as we drive."

Alex left the garage and headed for I-95 South.

"I'm not staying on the highway long," he said. "I think we'll be safer taking a longer route there, using back roads."

"That works for me."

They got off I-95 at the exit for T.F. Green Airport in Rhode Island and parked in the long-term parking lot. They waited for a car to pull in near them, and when the driver left with his suitcases, Alex switched the license plate with theirs. Alex explained that if the other person was parked in long-term parking and was just leaving for a flight now, they probably had at least a few days before the switch was discovered.

"You're getting good at this," said Hanna. "I wouldn't have thought of doing that here. But it makes sense."

"I guess you've corrupted me. How are you feeling?"

"Better. Not perfect, but it'll take time for the antibiotic to work. Before they knew that I was going to escape, they gave me 5-days' worth. It's getting rid of the Portal Sickness, though."

Hanna had made the transformation to Hanna Snow by donning a black shoulder-length wavy wig and blue-rimmed glasses.

"I can get by with the wig and glasses," she said, "that's easy. But eventually, you'll have to grow your hair, as well as your beard and mustache, and color them, so you don't have to fiddle with the fake ones every day."

They arrived at JFK Airport the next day. They didn't really have any place in mind, but a flight to Ireland caught their fancy. There were some seats available, so they took them.

"Most of our other travel from there can be by ship and then train," said Hanna. "We'll have to return and visit the others in eleven years. But for the next eleven years, let's take it slow and enjoy life."

"We deserve it," said Alex.

"We certainly do," replied Hanna.

"And it all starts now."

Chapter 48

OMAHA, NEBRASKA—1950

Nicholas had never seen New York City—at least from this era—and wanted to experience it. Besides, getting lost among millions of people couldn't hurt.

He was concerned about the assassins. How many were there? If they were able to track him, they had a definite advantage. On the other hand, if he could get his hands on one of the new Portal Finders, maybe it would give him the advantage of seeing them coming. Hanna had explained how they worked and how to look for the residue trails left by the travelers. All he had to do was to avoid getting killed first.

Nicholas wasn't one to show—or even feel—emotion, but he was sad to see Keith and Alice go. In his own way, he had formed a bond with them. They were a nice young couple, and he hoped that they would be able to have a good life together. It was something of which he had deprived himself. He had certainly had women in his life, but they were all one-night stands or fleeting relationships. Part of it was his job—a job that couldn't include relationships.

He blamed the job, but was it really more a case of not wanting to be tied down? Would the job have mattered when it came to relationships? Maybe it was just his personality. He was a loner by nature, and that's just how he preferred it.

He bought a train ticket to New York. It wasn't leaving for three hours, so he'd have to spend every minute watching his back. If the assassin, George, could find him, how many others followed that same residue trail? And how many assassins was he talking about? Two? Five? A dozen? That's what made it so hard—he could kill ten assassins and never know if there were more. That's why he needed one of the newer Portal Finders.

Nicholas left the bus station and found a diner around the corner. He was enjoying the food from this era. There was no comparison to the food he had grown up with. It was all fake—genetically modified fruits and vegetables, and meat that had very little actual meat in it.

He had time to kill, so he lingered over his cheeseburger and French fries, savoring every bite. But every second he sat there, he watched the other customers for any sign that they didn't belong. He had already seen that most people from the future displayed a certain awkwardness—probably himself included. Although he had spent his whole adult life blending in. He just had to look for those signs in the people around him. The other disadvantage for him was that all the assassins knew what he looked like.

It wasn't until he left the diner that he noticed the man. He was across the street holding a newspaper—the telltale sign of someone who doesn't know how to blend in.

Okay, he had spotted the man. Now he had to lure him into a trap.

He started walking in the opposite direction of the train station. He had to find a quiet spot to spring his trap, and hope that the assassin wasn't too anxious to finish the job.

There! Oh, it was perfect. A carnival was in full swing. It didn't cover an enormous area, but that was okay. It was large enough. He stopped at a popcorn stand and bought a bag. He took a few bites and realized that where he was from, popcorn was another genetically modified food that was tasteless compared to this. It was delicious!

Nicholas wandered the carnival, keeping his pursuer in sight at all times. However, the assassin became lazy, or anxious. Nicholas was rounding the corner of the bumper cars, when a piece of metal flew off a thick tent pole next to his head.

Not good!

There were too many families, too many children. What was the assassin thinking?

So far, no one had noticed it, thanks to the relative silence of the weapons. It didn't sound much different than a balloon bursting, if even that loud.

Nicholas raced around the back of a tent just as a hole appeared in the canvas.

This guy is too reckless, thought Nicholas.

He had his weapon but didn't want to shoot it around people. Besides, he needed to grab the man's backpack, which probably had one of the newer Portal Finders, and grab his weapon before someone got hurt.

Then he spied a row of eight portable toilets. As they were set further back from the carnival, there didn't seem to be anyone using them.

He looked behind him. If he worked fast, he might live through this. He entered the last toilet and closed the door. He set his weapon on "kill" and shot at the rear of the structure as fast as his finger would move, putting holes all around the edges. When he felt he had enough, he kicked the back wall. It almost gave in. He took a few more shots and kicked again. The back fell to the ground.

Nicholas jumped out the back and immediately hugged the ground. Suddenly, numerous pops were heard, and holes appeared in the structure's front door. Nicholas crawled around the side of the toilet.

The popping stopped, and the assassin opened the door. As he did, Nicholas, from a prone position, put three holes through the open door between him and the assassin. The door swung shut, and the man behind it dropped to the ground. There was no doubt that he was dead.

Nicholas had to work fast. He grabbed the man's backpack and weapon, and quickly checked his pockets, finding nothing of value.

He couldn't go back through the carnival—someone might have seen the exchange. Nicholas looked around. About fifty yards behind the line of toilets were the woods. That was his best option. He took off.

He was out of breath by the time he reached the trees. While he was in good shape for a man his age, the stress of the last few minutes had weakened him. He sat by a tree to catch his breath.

It seemed that no one had seen him running. That was good. Just then, a man came around the corner on his way to the toilets. He stopped, wide-eyed at the scene before him, then immediately turned and ran.

"Help! Someone call the cops! A man has been shot!"

That was Nicholas's cue to leave. Eventually, they would search the woods.

But what to do? Going back to the train station was out of the question. They'd be looking for someone escaping on a train.

As he had that thought, he heard a train whistle. Then he came out of the woods to a set of train tracks. He crossed the tracks and entered the woods on the other side. The train was approaching. It was a freight train. He remembered them from his childhood. Even early in the 22nd century, they still had them, although they had been modernized. But he remembered the old ones. He also recalled that some freight train cars left their sliding doors open.

The train was rumbling up the tracks at an excruciatingly slow speed—probably because it was entering a town.

Nicholas waited. There! A box car with an open door. It must have been empty. As it passed, Nicholas ran up the grade and grabbed onto a rung of a ladder. He pulled himself up and climbed into the dark car.

It took a moment for his eyes to adjust. In the corner were two men—men who looked like this was a normal form of travel for them.

"Mind if I share your car?"

"Hep yerself," said one of them. "Cost ya fifty bucks."

"Tell you what," said Nicholas. "I'll give you each fifty bucks if you promise to leave me alone."

"And if we don't?"

"I'll kill you."

The men looked at each other.

"You got yerself a deal."

"You've gotta come and get it. I'm too tired to stand up."

The two men stood up and cautiously approached Nicholas, who had pulled some bills from his pocket.

"All yours," he said. "Now, live up to your end of the bargain."

The men thanked him and scurried back to their spots.

And, as it turned out, the train was headed for New York.

It was time to get lost.

Chapter 49

BOSTON, MASSACHUSETTS—SEPTEMBER 2026

I had just returned from leaving the messages for Alex and Hanna about Keith and the others, Randy, and letting them know about the mass murderer. I had also stopped by Natalie's shoot in Toronto for a few more days. It was now Labor Day weekend, and they were taking a break from filming, so I convinced her to come home for the long weekend. It didn't take much convincing at all. She was anxious to go home for some quiet time and to see Hal and Simone.

We were having a barbeque in the backyard, the four of us together for the first time in ages. I had just gone inside for some ice when I heard the doorbell. I grabbed my gun and put it in my belt behind my back. With our notoriety, I couldn't be too careful.

I opened the door. It took me a second to process what I was seeing, and then my mouth hung open.

"Hi, Ray."

It was Alex and Hanna. They had aged at least ten years since I saw them last and looked to be in their early fifties—closer to my age. They had both changed their appearances, but there was no doubt that my old friends had arrived.

I reached out and hugged them.

"Lose your ability to speak?" asked Alex.

"I don't know what to say," I finally said. "I just left you the notes about Keith and the others a few days ago and got your response."

"That was almost twelve years ago," said Hanna. "A lot has happened."

"I have no doubt," I said. "Oh my God, it's so great to see you. I didn't know if we ever would. Everyone is in the backyard. You need to make your grand entrance."

I led them through the house. When I reached the backyard, I announced, "Visitors!"

The next few minutes were filled with tears and hugs as old friends were finally reunited. When things had died down, and Alex and Hanna had food and drink, they began their story.

"You were right, Simone, about the portals," said Hanna. "They are messed up. Five of us in three groups accessed the portal leading to 2030. We had to do it that way due to the size of the portal. We landed in 2015. We have no idea about the others. I guess we'll find out in 2030."

"Who were the others?" I asked.

"Before we tell you," said Hanna, "let me start by saying that we met the mass murderer, Nicholas Gates. It's a much more complicated story than the news led on. We'll tell you the full story later, but the short version is that we let him go. The last we heard, he was roaming 1950, with assassins on his trail. No, not Eliminators. Again, a story for a different time. Suffice to say, he's a good person. Your turn, Alex."

"We met Randy."

Natalie put her hand to her mouth. "He really lived?"

"He did. We got to him just in time. He had made the mistake of telling people he was from the future, and they put him in a mental institution. He traveled with us to 1950 and went through the portal. We hope he ended up in 2030 and can see his brother.

As for Keith and the others, Keith and Alice fell in love. You might not want to tell his wife. Again, we never saw them in 2015, so either they made it to 2030 or were sent somewhere else. If so, hopefully it was somewhere good, because they gave their Portal Finder to Nicholas."

"What about the other two?" I asked.

"Pete pissed off some people and was sent to France to fight in World War I. Alice said that Barbara joined the ambulance corps in hopes of seeing Pete. I guess they were in love. That's the end of the trail."

"I might go online and see if I can find them in the lists from World War I," I said. "It's mainly out of curiosity."

"And what about you two?" asked Simone. "What have you been doing for eleven years?"

"We've been surviving," said Hanna.

"Mostly, we've been traveling," said Alex. "It took me a while to learn this complicated new world. Hanna caught Portal Sickness and almost died."

That got a gasp from the group.

"It turns out that a common antibiotic was enough to cure it. The doctors are still stumped about what it could be. The fun part of all this was watching you guys. Every once in a while, we returned to the States. While we were here, we'd check in on you. Hal was the easiest to watch; his routine was the most boring."

"Gee, thanks," said Hal.

"We also watched the other travelers who came to your place of work: Herb, Alan, Uncle Jim, and the famous Stan Hooper, who started all this. Because Ray hadn't yet gone back in time, we didn't feel comfortable connecting with any of them. We didn't know how time would be affected."

"I made one exception to that," said Hanna. "I knew from you, Ray, that Uncle Jim was sick and dying. After you went out west, I visited Jim. I had to. If you remember, he wasn't just a coworker; he really was my uncle. I had to see him before he died. It was a great reunion. While I was there, Alan came in. I made him promise not to tell you that he had seen me. Again, I don't know what the repercussions would have been. I guess it didn't matter. Alan was killed soon after."

"When you all came home last year," said Alex, "we kept an eye on you, just waiting for this moment. By then, we had moved back here permanently. We saw your speech on TV, Natalie, from Vermont, after you showed up. Great speech."

"Thanks."

"We had to wait until now to make our presence known," said Hanna. "We had to wait until you returned from sending your last note to us."

"It's so strange to know that I just sent you the notes," I said, "but for you, it was almost twelve years ago. It boggles the mind."

"It does," said Hanna. "This last year was tough, knowing we were so close, and we tried to stay patient. But as Alex said, we've been doing a lot of traveling. Seeing the world without the stress of moving on to a different time has been wonderful."

"And I'm up to date on all the technology," said Alex. "It wasn't easy bringing my 1970s mind into 2015 and beyond. But I succeeded. I've also caught up on all the movies since the 1970s, including all of yours, Natalie. You're really good."

"Thank you."

"And," continued Alex, "Hanna has seen all my favorites from before I left the 1970s."

"A lot of them are kind of cheesy," said Hanna.

"Cheesy?" asked Natalie.

"Alex taught me the word."

We spent hours talking and laughing. They went into more detail about Nicholas Gates, Randy, Keith, and Alice. I knew I would have to speak to Cyndi at some point, but was hoping that Simone might want to do it for me. I'm such a coward.

Alex and Hanna were now living in Maine, so they accepted our invitation to stay with us for a few days before heading home.

*****

The next morning, I got on the computer and looked up the list of deaths from World War I. It took a while, but I eventually found Pete and Barbara. Peter Green and Barbara Cox, both of North Conway, New Hampshire, were listed among the dead. It saddened me to know that their lives had turned out that way.

Alex told me the story they had heard from Keith about Bill and Ruth Hobbs, of the Mountain Vista Inn, so just for fun, I looked them up. Bill died in 1930. Ruth remained the owner for another ten years before selling it when the Great Depression ended. She died in 1957 at the age of ninety. I wondered what happened when the other four missing hotel workers showed up through the portal. I could only guess that they were treated better than Pete was.

As for Randy, Keith, and Alice, we just had to hope they landed someplace good. Hanna had tracked two trails to 1974 but didn't know if they belonged to Keith and Alice. Did any of them make it to 2030?

Only time would tell.

Chapter 50

As it turns out, the appearance of Alex and Hanna wasn't my only surprise.

The next day, I received a phone call.

"Is this Mr. Burton?" A female voice. A *nervous* female voice.

"It is."

"I'm wondering if my brother and I can meet with you."

"What is it you'd like to meet about?"

"We'd rather tell you in person. But let's just say that we've been waiting over twenty years to meet you. We also have a message to give you. Our instructions were very specific. We couldn't contact you before August 15, 2026."

Okay, she had my attention. That was the day Keith and the others went through the portal.

"I'm free now if you'd like to come by."

"We'll be there in ten minutes. We're right down the road in a gas station parking lot. We were hoping you'd be available."

Natalie was still home, not scheduled to return to Toronto until the next day, so I told her about our visitors. Alex and Hanna were also curious. I thought that Hal and Simone should be part of this since it obviously involved time travel, so I called them and was told they'd be there in five minutes.

So, we were all sitting in the living room when the doorbell rang. I opened the door and looked at twins—a man and a woman a few years younger than me. Both were blonde and about 5'10". Both were so nervous they were almost shaking.

"Hi, I'm Ray."

"Hi, Ray. I can't believe we are finally here. This is a big deal for us. No, this is massive. My name is Barbara, and my brother is Pete."

"Barbara and Pete?" I asked incredulously.

"We were named after our mom's friends," said Pete. "The names might be familiar to you."

"Of course they are," I said. "Please come in."

They followed me into the living room and stopped short at the sight of so many people. I introduced them all and explained that everyone there was connected to time travel.

"Which is why you came, I assume."

"It is," said Barbara. "Our parents were Keith and Alice, who went through the portal in New Hampshire."

"Oh my god!" said Hanna. "I'm Hanna, and this is Alex. We traveled with them for a time."

"Yes, they spoke a lot about you. They were very fond of you."

"And we were of them."

"For you," Barbara said to me, "it was only a month ago that they went through. For us, it happened a few years before we were born. Our dad died in 2020 at the age of 81. Our mom died last year. She was 75. When we were thirty, our parents decided to share their story with us. At first, we didn't believe a word of it, but then they presented various forms of proof. Finally, we had to accept that what they told us was true—that we might be the first children of time travelers."

"You might not be the first," I said. "There's no way we can know that. But you are certainly the first to come forward. If there are others, they probably don't know that they are. I lost contact with Keith and the others the same day I put the notes in the portal. That was a month ago. I know that they landed in 1917. I know they made it to 1950, because they were with Alex and Hanna.

"They did go to 1950," said Barbara, "From there, a portal was supposed to take them to 2030."

"We were with them," said Hanna. "We all had to go through that portal. But it was so small that only two people could go through at once. Using our advanced Portal Finder, we tracked a couple of people to 1974. Was that them?"

"Yes. They told us that they had been warned about it. They had also given the Portal Finder to Nicholas, who had no interest in going to 2030."

"We ended up in 2015," said Alex. "We don't know where Randy went. Hopefully, he made it—or will make it—to 2030. I guess we won't know until then."

"It was hard for them," said Pete, "but they said it also solved a problem. By coming back to 2030, our dad would have to choose between his wife, Cyndi, whom he still loved, and our mom, whom he had also fallen in love with. He asked us to visit Cyndi after we saw you. Do you think it's a good idea?"

I deferred to Natalie.

"I think it would be nice to do that," she said. "It would give her some closure and allow her to move on with her life while she's still young. However, I wouldn't mention anything about the dilemma your father was going to face if he came back in 2030. Just tell her that he always missed her but had to get on with his life. Let her know that it's also what he wanted for her."

"I can pave the way for you to see her," I said.

"And Alex and I can go with you," said Hanna. "We got to know them. Maybe it will help somehow."

"I'll go, too," said Simone. "I've talked to Cyndi a few times in the last week."

"Thank you," said Barbara.

"Tell us about your parents," I said.

"They were very happy together," said Barbara. "When they arrived in 1974, they had a little money. They said it was thanks to Alex. Knowing the future, our father invested some of it in the stock market, knowing which stocks would become valuable. He also bought sports cards that he knew would be valuable later on. When Apple went public, he was right there, ready to invest. My parents became millionaires just from that investment alone. Over the years, at the direction of our parents, we've bought up collectibles of all kinds. And we've invested in companies they knew would take off, so we and our families are also financially set."

"They said they were scared when they first got to 1974, especially knowing that they were stuck there," said Pete, "but once they got used to it, they liked it. They said it was a simpler time, and since they already knew what would happen, they could adjust accordingly. They blended into the background. They changed their names. They didn't even want to check out their parents as young people or view themselves as children."

"Probably smart," said Hanna.

"When you disappeared in 2009, Natalie, my parents knew what had happened, but couldn't say anything without sounding like crackpots. That's the year they told us about time travel. They said it was a very surreal time for them. We're just sorry that our parents didn't live to see Alex and Hanna again, or to meet you, Ray."

"It is," I answered. "Even after all that I've witnessed, I still find it amazing that since they went through the portal, I've lived a month, and they lived close to fifty years. It's why time travel is such a scary concept."

"I wouldn't want to wish it on anyone," said Hal.

"Our father wrote a book detailing his experiences," said

Barbara. "He wanted us to give it to you to read before we tried to publish it. We don't need the money, but it was important to him. It was also important to him that you approve it."

"I'd be happy to read it," I said. "And maybe some of the others would like to read it, too."

Hal, Alex, and Hanna all nodded their heads. I was aware that Natalie had refrained. I didn't blame her—she was trying her hardest to leave time travel behind.

We talked for a while longer, and then Simone called Cyndi and told her she was coming by with some people to talk to her about Keith.

*****

As for me? I'm done researching time travel and time travelers. I'm not sure what my next step will be. I'm considering going on location with Natalie whenever she makes a movie. That way, Natalie will still be able to act, but we'll be together, which is all we've ever wanted.

What'll I do when she's filming?

Hey, maybe I'll write a novel—something NOT related to time travel!

Epilogue

NEW YORK CITY—1950

The neon sign outside his hotel room hissed and buzzed all night, keeping Nicholas awake. He had shut the broken blinds enough to keep most of the red and blue lights from reflecting off his walls, but the buzzing was constant. He lay on the lumpy mattress, staring at the ceiling.

Who was he kidding? He wasn't going to sleep. It wasn't the buzzing keeping him awake—it was the assassins. He had encountered two of them—George, and the man at the carnival—but he knew there were more. How many? That was the question he didn't think he'd ever know the answer to. It meant that he could never relax—he would always be looking over his shoulder.

He had considered ending it. It would be so easy. Just a shot to the chest, and it would be all over. If he did it on the water, the Portal Finder and weapon would sink to the bottom, never to be found.

But he wasn't ready to die. He had been given a gift. He had a Portal Finder. He had destroyed the Portal Finder given to him by Keith and Alice, as he now had a more advanced one. With that, he could go anywhere he wanted. He should make the most of it. Nicholas had led a hard life in a hard time back in the 22nd

century. He now had the opportunity to relax and enjoy life, or he would have if not for the assassins following him. The trouble was, he couldn't see them coming. They could be anywhere. He thought that traveling to New York would be good. He could blend into the woodwork.

He sat up suddenly.

Maybe that was the wrong idea!

He hadn't been thinking clearly. He didn't need to blend into the woodwork in a large city. He needed to go somewhere with wide open spaces where he could see his attacker coming. He had to get out of the city.

Nicholas already had several advantages over those who were looking for him. He had been doing this for a lifetime—hiding and hunting. After all, he was a professional killer. He was also smart. The men following him were, by nature, stupid. They were greedy men who were conned into going back in time without a clear understanding of how to return home. He also now had the newer Portal Finder—thanks to the assassin from the carnival—which might help him find them.

He'd leave in the morning. He'd head west. In retrospect, he should have stayed in Nebraska. But he wanted to see New York. There, he'd seen it. It was time to move on.

His door flew open, and he heard a pop, then another and another. His pillow had three holes in it. But Nicholas wasn't there. He might've been old, but he still had great reflexes. The minute the door was kicked open, he was on the floor.

He jumped up and attacked. The man in the doorway wasn't expecting it. He peered into the dark to see if he had killed his target. Thoughts of a $5 million bonus were already floating around his brain.

Nicholas slammed into his attacker, sending him flying into the hallway. The man's head made a hole in the thin wall.

Nicholas continued his assault on the assassin, punching and kicking him with a speed that left the man unable to defend himself. The attacker was dazed, so Nicholas stepped back and kicked him in the head. The man slumped to the ground. Nicholas grabbed him by the ankles and quickly pulled him into the room.

He had to work fast.

He tore off the man's backpack and pulled out his Portal Finder and weapon. He checked for anything else he'd need. In the man's pocket was $200. Hey, every little bit helped.

Nicholas added the man's Portal Finder and weapon to his backpack, then shot him twice in the heart.

He heard noises in the hallway. Someone was coming to check on the commotion. It was time to go. He opened the door. The desk clerk from downstairs was examining the hole in the wall. He turned quickly when he heard Nicholas open the door.

"What happened here? You know you're going to have to pay for it."

Nicholas ignored him and headed down the hallway.

*****

A week later, Nicholas was walking along a dirt road in Oklahoma. His Portal Finder showed a portal in Colorado that went back to the 1880s. That might be interesting. From there? Who knew? Maybe he'd check out Europe or Asia. Maybe South America.

He had so much to see.

And the rest of his life to see it.

The End

ABOUT THE AUTHOR

Andrew Cunningham is the author of 18 novels, including the *"Lies" Mystery Series*: **All Lies, Fatal Lies, Vegas Lies, Secrets & Lies, Blood Lies, Buried Lies,** and **Sea of Lies;** the post-apocalyptic *Eden Rising Series*: **Eden Rising, Eden Lost, Eden's Legacy,** and **Eden's Survival**; the *Yestertime Time Travel Series:* **Yestertime, The Yestertime Effect, The Yestertime Warning,** and **The Yestertime Shift;** the disaster/terrorist thriller **Deadly Shore,** and the *Alaska Thrillers:* **Wisdom Spring** and **Nowhere Alone.** As A.R. Cunningham, he has written a series of five children's mysteries in the *Arthur MacArthur* series. Born in England, Andrew was a long-time resident of Cape Cod. He and his wife now live in Florida. Please visit his website at *arcnovels.com*, or his Facebook page, *Author Andrew Cunningham*.

Made in the USA
Las Vegas, NV
18 December 2023